HORR

Volume 1

(Hauntings)

Edited by Colin C. Martin

HORRORific Tales

HORRORific Tales Volume 1 (Hauntings)

Paperback Edition ISBN 978-1-0684637-4-7

Published by HORRORific Productions Ltd
61 Bridge Street, Kington, Herefordshire,
HR5 3DJ, England, United Kingdom

A CIP catalogue number for this title is available from the British Library

This book is dedicated to independent creators trying to make their way in the world. By honing your craft and not taking the easy payout from the bland, sterile corporations you inspire us, spark our imaginations and make us believe that anything is possible. Keep striving on your journey, stay true to yourself and may every success that you deserve arrive at your door.

Special thanks to Cameron, Chris, Del and FL_3 for being my co-hosts, inner circle and close support as I've went on this creative journey. Here's to the beginning of something truly HORRORific!

Thank you also to the myriads of independent creators who have interacted with our podcast and publisher over the years. You have helped to inspire me to keep going and to put something out into the world.

Hauntings can manifest in many ways. A restless spirit can become tethered to our realm, unable to cross over and find eternal peace. Often related to their demise an entity can find itself attached to a location, object, person or even a memory. Unable to complete their journey a spirit will plead with, cry out to or lash out at the living. We explore a few of these occurrences in this collection of tales.

Contents

Introduction

I started The HORRORific Podcast with a simple idea. Read out a few stories from authors while having a bit of fun playing around with sound effects and music, then once or twice a month catch up with my buddy Cameron to chat about movies and goings on in the horror genre. What I wasn't expecting was for this thing to take on a life of its own and blow up like it did. Over four years and thousands of videos and streams later I've interviewed a wide range of creators, built friendships and networks with other channels played games and generally had a blast whilst building this platform.

It isn't all fun and games being a creator as you know. The hours of administration in the background, trying to navigate the various social media trends and algorithms just to try and get a foothold on the landscape. Learning about and trying to keep up to date with the technology required to bring digital content to life and that's before we even get to the random trolls and people who want to tear you down just for trying.

There have been a couple of times over the years when I've nearly hit the wall, coming close to burnout and giving up. That's when you, my friends and supporters have always managed to step in at the right time and pick me up again. Be it a kind comment, sharing a post or mentioning me in one of your works. It's all been noticed and appreciated and reminds me that the art of creation is a positive and worthwhile endeavour.

I've always had it in the back of my mind to put together something tangible to show my support for artists trying to make their mark on the world and this first volume of HORRORific Tales is the start of that journey. If you are reading this, it is likely that you have already listened to and watched some of the authors featured on the podcast and I'd like to extend my heartfelt thanks for continuing to support us by picking up this publication.

If you have just arrived and came across this book first, then let me take a moment to welcome you and invite you to join us as we continue to discuss horror and the journey of being a creator whilst having a little fun along the way!

That just leaves me to say. Until next time my friends. Remember to Keep it creepy, keep it HORRORific!

Yours in appreciation

Colin

The HORRORific Podcast is available on numerous platforms. Find us where you usually get your podcasts here:

HORRORific Tales

A House on Maple Drive

by
Katie Marie

When we turned onto Maple Drive, dad squirmed with glee. The houses were enormous; the road was smooth and spotless, and expensive looking cars filled long driveways. “Rein it in a bit” I nudged him as I pulled into Mrs Turing’s drive. He scoffed at me and all but leapt out of the door. I turned to look at the boys in the back of the van. Jasper smirked, and Ryan offered a shrug that communicated his amused ambivalence. I sighed and stepped out of the van.

Mrs Turing’s house was a beast. I craned my neck to take it in. Ryan let out a whistle beside me. “Couldn’t have parked closer?” Jasper said. “We’re gonna have to get all the gear up there.” “The exercise will do you good.” I muttered before jogging up the drive to catch up with dad. When I reached him, the skeletal Mrs Turning was doddering out of the house.

“Oh! Mr Gravestone,” Mrs Turing lifted her arms as she shuffled at top speed towards my dad. Her voice was loud, and I couldn’t help but notice her glance at the surrounding homes. Her volume increased when one of the neighbouring curtains twitched. “I’m so glad you made it!”

She wobbled dramatically and mock stumbled. Dad, ever the knight in shining armour, caught her before she could fall.

“Of course, Mrs Turing, we dropped everything to be here for you.” He got her steady on her feet. Under the gaudy shawl she was stick thin and frail. She put me in mind of a bird, covered in colourful feathers but light and fragile beneath them. “Oh, I wouldn’t want to put you in any trouble.” Her grin said otherwise. “Not at all,” dad said. “You remember my daughter Rose?” Mrs Turing looked at me and nodded. “Yes, dear, thank you so much for coming out all this way.” Her smile was sticky sweet.

“No trouble at all, mam.” I dipped my head ever so slightly. “Do you mind if we come in and look around? I need to tell the boys where they need to set up.” “Oh, of course,” Mrs Turing took dad’s arm and started back into the house. “Do come in.”

Evidence of a life lived richly overfilled the house. Paintings and photographs covered every wall. Ornaments litter every table. Every room felt like a museum to this woman’s life.

"You've lived a fascinating life, Mrs Turing." Dad picked up a photograph of her and her late husband at the pyramids. "You must have some wonderful stories to tell."

"Oh, I could entertain you for weeks, Mr Gravestone." Mrs Turing laughed, the sound hearty despite her frail frame. "Please call me Jim," Dad allowed us to be led upstairs. "Only if you'll call me Madeleine, Jim." Mrs Turing smiled, placing a hand on his chest, "My hero in my hour of need." "Let's not get ahead of ourselves, Madeleine." Dad laughed. "But goodness, this house is beautiful." "Yes, well Roger, God rest him. He inherited it from his aunt, you see. Her husband's family was on paper and, well, the rest is history."

I kept my hand on the dark wood banister as I followed them, paying close attention to the photos on the wall. The couple had travelled everywhere, but they had done so alone by the looks of it, no pictures of other family, just them. In every picture, her late husband, Roger, always had his arm around her waist and a drink in his other hand. She always dressed lavishly, appearing a little too perfect.

“This is Roger’s study; I have moved nothing.” Mrs Turing unlocked a door and led us into a dark room. “All the um, activity, has been happening in here. So, I locked the door, closed the curtains and hoped it would stop.” She started opening curtains as she spoke. “But nothing stopped. It’s got worse.” “Worse how?” Dad helped her open curtains. “Well, it’s moved all over the house.

Yesterday I heard the most dreadful bang from the basement and the poor delivery boy who brings in my shopping each week, well he had the accident just last week.”

“Oh?” I frowned. “You mentioned nothing about this before.” Mrs Turing shuffled uncomfortably under my gaze. “I was afraid if it was too frightening, you might not come, and I so desperately need your help.” Her eyes grew wet, and I had to fight rolling my eyes at her. “What happened?” dad took her hand. “Well, Roger, he never liked when other men looked at me. He was possessive, you see.” Mrs Turing sniffed and wiped at a dry eye. “And the delivery boy is very handsome.”

“What happened?” I said, it was a little firmer. Dad shot me a hard look. “He was putting away my rice and the shelf at the top of the store. Roger must have loosened it, because the whole thing came down. Knocking the poor boy unconscious, I panicked. I was so frightened. I had to run next door for help. They called an ambulance. The paramedic wanted to take me in, but I said no.” “What about the delivery boy?” I said. “Oh, he was fine. A bump on the head is all.” Mrs Turing looked up at dad. “But I was ever so frightened!” “I see.” I said. “Why don’t you get set up in here, Rose, and we’ll go investigate the kitchen,” Dad said, sending me another hard look when Mrs Turin turned away.

I nodded and headed out to update the boys on where we were setting up.

As I was walking behind dad and Mrs Turning, the old woman stopped just outside of the kitchen. Her expression changed from the pleasant smile and turned stern. “I want you to check all the house.” She said strongly, she looked at me. “That includes the rooms upstairs, the attic, and the basement.” “We’ll be thorough.” I nodded. Her eyes stayed on me hard. “Make sure that you are. I’m trusting you with this.”

It wasn't until 7pm that we were fully set up and dad managed to get a fussing Mrs Turing to leave. She'd be staying in a local hotel for the night while we carried out our work. Officially, we did this so we could get unbiased results. Honestly, we did it so that the client couldn't see what we were doing.

"Old witch looks like a miniature Cruella Deville," Jasper laughed over his plastic container of noodles. "At least Cruella had fashion sense." Ryan laughed. "You two are such bitches," I snorted, discarding the remains of my dinner into the takeaway bag. "Oh, come on," Jasper grumbled. "You can't pretend it's not true." "That doesn't mean you have to say it." "Like you're not thinking the same thing."

Ryan took a long sip of his drink and glanced at the workstation. It looked impressive. Multiple screens, some running numbers, one resembled a radar, others showed a live video feed that we would edit later. I shrugged.

"There's so much you could give her a hard time about; her fashion choice isn't where I'd start." "Picky, picky," Ryan sighed and turned to Jasper. "I recon we could rig something at the desk, maybe the bookcase?" "Bookcase?" Jasper rolled his eyes. "Again, with the books?" "Books falling is what people expect," Ryan snapped back. "Especially if we can find an old diary or something." "What'd you find?" Jasper turned to me.

"At the moment, just a bunch of photos showing that her husband was a drinker. They travelled and don't seem to be close to the rest of the family. I'll go have another look around, see if I can find anything better." I got to my feet and headed out of the study. I picked up a handheld camera on my way. "I'll get some footage of the rest of the house while I'm at it. See if there's anything you can use later." "Thanks, kiddo." Jasper called over his shoulder.

The upper floors comprised a couple of guest bedrooms, Mrs Turing's bedroom, and an enormous bathroom. The bathroom was bigger than my entire apartment. I rummaged through some drawers in each of the rooms but there were no secret diaries, no saved newspapers, nothing beyond overpriced clothes, cosmetics and toiletries. Downstairs told much the same story, though it was slightly more interesting. The dining room at least had a display of family history, showing how the old family had made the move into paper. The dining room had various awards for business achievements and a few old newspapers framed to showcase milestones in the business history. Roger's aunt had done well to marry into this. I'd researched the family before we arrived and had found that Roger, Mr Turing, had inherited not only the house, but his aunt's share in the business. He'd been a smart man who'd not just sat on his thumbs, he'd actively grown the business, moving from shareholder to board director in five short years. He'd stayed as director until he retired. Then, only two years after retirement, he'd died of a heart attack. Mrs Turin had found his body in the basement.

I was about to head into the basement when Dad came in through the door grumbling to himself. "You ok?" I turned the camcorder off. "Stuck-up bitch," dad grumbled. "Turned down the first two hotels we went to, I wouldn't mind, but she booked the damn thing. Finally got her to accept a room at the Maid's Head County Park. Damn tempted to charge her for the bloody petrol." "I thought it was taking you a while to drop her off." I chuckled; dad glared at me. "That's not what's really bothering you though, is it?" Dad sighed and shook his head.

"She's the only lead that turned out to be worth anything out of the last five shows." "The shows bring in enough on their -," I started, dad held up his hand. "No, they don't. The shows are supposed to bring in clients. If they aren't doing that then, maybe it's me, maybe I …" he trailed off.

"You're not losing your mojo," I went and wrapped my arms around him. "You're still the best in the biz. Hell, you convinced the richest woman in god knows how far that her dead husband was haunting her." "She just wants the attention," dad pushed me gently away. "She knows this is bullshit." "No, she doesn't," I stepped back. "She was eating out of your hand." Dad smiled a little. "Maybe," he said.

“But you gotta find us something good. There’s only so much magic I can spin on my own.” “It’s hardly magic, but I’ll do my best.”

I headed back to the basement door. “The boys are upstairs. I ordered you a Chow Mein. Better go up before Jasper steals it.” I watched dad go upstairs before opening the door to the basement.

It was exhausting to feed his ego every single time we did this, but it was worth it. He was good at what he did. He could charm the gold right out of a man’s pocket and as a result we lived pretty well. We provided a service to those who needed a little more out of life than what life gave them. We brought magic and mysticism into their lives, faith and belief. If we charged a modest fee and exaggerated our results, then it was only as much as we needed to. The shows usually got fully booked months in advance, and in the crowd, I’d find the best marks. I was good at reading people, though most people don’t make it hard. In the interval, I’d told dad which ones to focus on and he’d put just enough spin and showmanship into his words that after the show we’d always be approached by one or two people who needed our ‘help’. Help we’d gladly provide, for a price.

The basement was well lit and clean. Had I not just gone down a flight of stairs, I'd never know I was in a basement. Like the rest of the house, it was a museum to the lives of Roger and Madeleine. The only difference to upstairs was that this museum was in boxes. I groaned to myself and started rummaging. It was gone 11pm when I found something interesting.

I found a small wooden box, different from the other plastic ones. Someone had hidden it away instead of placing it on one of the well-organised shelving units. This one was in a filing cabinet hidden behind two other filing cabinets. It was in the bottom drawer and was an absolute bitch to get out. It was also locked. "Oh, well." I muttered, pulling my lock picks out of my pocket. "I wish someone had grown up in a family of con artists and crooks." I had the box open in minutes. "Jackpot." I took the box upstairs.

"Well, you look like the cat that caught the canary," Ryan said when I walked in. "Oh, thank god," Jasper grinned. "Please tell me you got something good, otherwise I'm gonna have to go with Ryan's terrible ideas." "I got something good." I held up the box. "We got ourselves an adulterous husband." "Oh, that is good," dad took the box away from me and started rifling through it.

“This is gold.” “So we what?” Ryan said. “Stage the haunting as him trying to come clean with his wife?”

“Sounds good,” I nodded. “I got some footage of the basement I’m sure you can use; Ryan and I can go film some more.” I glanced at dad. “But I bet she’d like it best if it was you who Roger ‘spoke’ to.”

Dad didn’t look up at me. He was staring down into the book; a sweat had broken out on his forehead and all the colour had drained from his face, making him look ghost white. “Dad?” I said. “Jim?” Ryan flicked a spring roll at dad. That got his attention. He snapped the box closed and let out a thin chuckled. “Oh yeah, um, great idea.” He looked at me, the whites of his eyes showing. “Um, where…” He swallowed as if his throat were dry. “Where did you find this?” “I’ll show you.” I stood up, observing him. Something in the box had upset him, but dad was a strange guy. He could smile through some of the darkest family secrets we’d unearthed, only to fall apart when it became apparent someone missed their childhood dog.

I led Ryan and dad down to the basement while Jasper worked his video editing magic on the footage we'd already got. The basement was as I had left it, sterile and feeling like the least haunted basement in England. "It's in the cabinet behind these," I walked over and started clambering over cabinets to get to the one right at the back where someone had hidden the box.

Dad, however, wasn't following. He'd gone to a wall lined with shelving units and started pulling boxes down. "Jim?" Ryan asked. Dad said nothing, just kept pulling boxes down. The wall behind the shelves, much like the rest of the walls in the basement, was painted white, giving the impression of space and cleanliness.

I gave up trying to show dad where I'd found the box and instead went to where he'd put it on the shelf. Opening it, I leafed through the pictures. Most of them were of women in various states of undress. Most of them were recognisable in the bedroom upstairs. Some were harder to tell though, the pictures close ups, so the background wasn't in it so much.

At the bottom of the box was an envelope, in the envelope were more pictures. The first one was of a woman, topless in front of a door. The walls were a different colour, but the light fittings were the same. It was the basement. I glanced at where dad was still pulling boxes off shelves. Ryan was helping now. Looking back at the photos, I dropped the box.

The rest of the photos looked like a studio; they were more graphic than the previous bedroom glamour shots. The women were younger than well. Some had bruises, others were restrained, and all appeared visibly frightened. I stopped looking before I got to the bottom of the pile. I didn't need to see; I needed to help.

Dad and Ryan had cleared the shelving unit. Behind it, painted white to match the walls, was the door. "Holy shit." I breathed. Dad turned around to look at me. "You can go back upstairs, sweetheart, get Jasper. We'll need help to move this." "Hell no," I went and grabbed the shelving unit. "I'm not going anywhere."

Together, we pulled and the unit slowly came away from the wall. I used my pocketknife to cut through the paint around the door. Even with the paint cut, the door was impossible to open until Ryan noted a painted over lock. It took me an hour to pick the paint out of the lock and force it to give under my lock picks. Once open, the door revealed Mr Turning's private studio.

When Mrs Turing returned to her home the following morning, it immediately became apparent that she knew what we would find. She arrived in a private hire car, not content with waiting for dad to go and find her and she smiled when she saw the police cars. I couldn't help but go over to her as a policeman helped her into one of their cars.

"You knew." I said, it wasn't a question. "I knew about Roger's little hobbies, yes," she said, her smiled still in place. "I promised I wouldn't do anything until after he was gone. But those families have the right to know what happened." I stepped back away from the car as the police officer put a hand on my shoulder and drew me away.

Follow Katie and her work here:

The lady in the Mirror

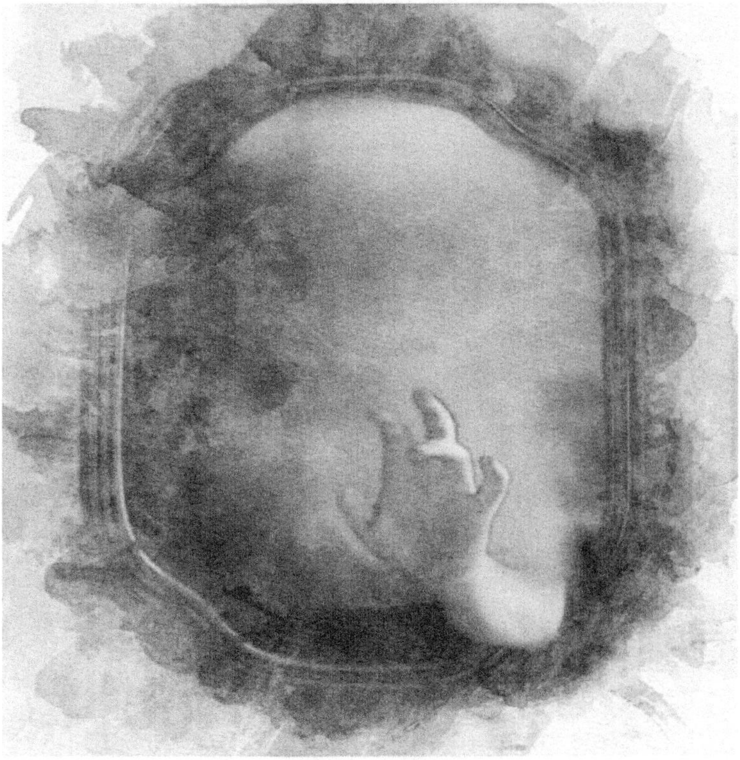

by Del Gibson

Regan and I finally make it to the cabin in the woods as twilight explodes across the landscape in hues of golds and reds. From the porch the view of the forest goes on and on forever; it's breathtaking.

"There better bloody be power and an indoor loo!" I say, in a grump because of the four-hour trek through the forest. "I suppose at least the view makes up for the time it took to get here."

"Alice, stop bitching. You used to love hiking, are you getting too old?" Regan laughs.

"Thirty-five is not old, you're older than me. No, it's not that; you silly man," I say, looking at the darkening sky, then to my husband of five years. "I just don't like this forest, I've heard too many terrible stories online about it, and a few YouTubers have done paranormal investigations here too. Also, people have gone missing in these woods and have never been heard from again."

"Whatever. You do know they make those tales up to scare you? It's all fake, just for views."

He opens the door and switches on the lights to prove there is power, then we take a quick tour. It's a lovely wood cabin with a big glass window in the living room, with a snug open fire in the corner, and there's a sliding door that goes out to the deck; a kitchen with a four-person dinner table; two bedrooms, and one bathroom with a working toilet – thank God it's not a long-drop! It's nothing too grand, just an ordinary cabin.

But it's deathly cold in here, I can see my breath when I exhale.

Regan lights a fire to disperse some of the chill, and I boil the kettle to make hot chocolates. Sitting in front of the flames is so comfortable that my body has finally relaxed after the day trekking. I feel the rush of sleep overcome me.

"Goodnight honey, I'm off to bed." I yawn. "Please don't be too long, this place is giving me the heebie-jeebies. It's so dark and isolated out here."

"Okay, I'll be there soon," Regan replies.

I climb into bed, it feels nice enough, but the mattress is a little too firm.

Sometime later, I hear the bedroom door creak open. I look up from my book, thinking it's my husband.

I ask, "Have you remembered to lock all the doors?" I wait for a reply that doesn't come. "Regan, is that you?"

My eyes scan the room but he's not there.

Trying to sleep is useless so I go out to the living room to ask him why he came into the bedroom and didn't say anything, but he's fast asleep snoring on the couch.

"Fine. Whatever, sleep out here then." I hear venom leak from my words. I leave him there and return to bed.

In the middle of the night, I'm woken by a strange noise that sounds like loud banging, though it could be thunder, but it's not raining. Looking out the bedroom window to check, the sky is alight with millions of dazzling stars, and no storm in sight. Puzzled, I go and investigate. Regan is no longer in the living room. I search everywhere inside the cabin but it's like he's disappeared. Fortunately, I find him standing outside on the deck in the freezing cold, shivering, and staring out towards the forest.

"What the hell are you doing out here? Come inside before you catch your death!"

When I don't get a response, I give him a shove and he seems to come back to himself.

"Why am I out here?" he asks, looking dazed.

I drag him by the arm back inside the cabin. We get into bed and it's toastie because I left the electric blanket going.

"Why were you outside? And why did you come into the bedroom?"

His teeth chatter when he answers, “I don’t recall coming in here. I’m not sure why I was outside either. First, I heard dogs barking somewhere in the distance, and the next thing I knew you were waking me up.”

“Perhaps you were sleepwalking?” I suggest. I feel his body finally heat up beside me. “Let’s talk about it in the morning. Goodnight,” I say, drifting off.

I wake to screams ripping me from my sleep. I soon realise it’s me screaming through a nightmare. *I’m running through the woods away from Regan. He’s chasing me with an axe and laughing diabolically.*

The digital clock says it’s 3:33am. Regan isn’t beside me. *Perhaps he’s in the loo?* I pull on a sweatshirt and jeans and go searching for him. The wooden floor is bitter cold beneath my naked feet. I wander around, switching on the lights as I go. Anxiety grips me because I can’t find him anywhere. I’m about to get on warmer clothes so that I can search outside, but I hear his voice, and so I follow.

I discover him in the back of the hallway closet where the cleaning supplies and equipment are stored. He's mumbling to himself and clutching a large kitchen knife in his hand; the one I used tonight for dinner, and it still has salad attached to it.

"Regan, what the hell are you doing in here?"

His eyes are closed and his incoherent mutterings increase – it looks like he's fighting someone in his dream.

"I said to stay away from me, or I'll cut you up!" he screams.

"Regan, you're having a nightmare. Wake up!" I shake him, even though I know you're not supposed to wake those in the throes of a night-terror.

It takes a few seconds until his eyes open, but they're too wide; it's unnatural. The fright sends me flying backwards, bumping my back against the hallway wall. The torment screwing up his features into a macabre mask, makes him look like he's seen a ghost.

His eyes are black not blue. I stand outside the door, trembling in fear as I watch intrigued when his eyes return to normal.

A loud bang behind me has me scrambling to my feet. I feel a presence watching me, but when I turn to look, there's nobody there. All of the lights in the cabin flicker on and off as I gently help my husband to his feet, but he's weak and he has to lean against the door frame to right himself. I direct him back to bed, and eventually we fall asleep.

In the morning I'm dragged back to consciousness by the smell of bacon and eggs – it draws me into the kitchen.

Regan's lips taste sweet when we kiss.

"That smells delicious darling. Yes please, and a big cup of tea to go with it," I say, sniffing in the wonderful scent of a cooked breakfast.

While we eat, we chat about last night's events. Regan only remembers bits of it, and I'm trying hard to forget. We decide it'll be a good idea to hike over to the lake, for a change of scenery. Nature has a way of clearing out the system and refreshing my mind.

Regan was offered this cabin by the owner, who is a client of his, though he can't tell me who because of patient confidentiality, so he says. He's a psychologist at the women state prison, he helps inmates through therapy, rehabilitation, before they're released back into the community. It's wonderful for me to be out of the classroom for a bit; teaching creative writing at the college is great though. I love my job.

With a picnic lunch packed, it takes us an hour to reach the lake. The sun is glowing hot rays in the cloudless sky. The lake is crystal clear when we reach it.

After a while, I've had enough of laying on the sunbaked sand, I leave Regan to his magazine, dip my toes in, and the water's tepid.

"I'm going in. I want to get to the pontoon."

"Okay Ali, I might join you soon."

When the water reaches my stomach, I dive in, shrieking when I emerge; a joyous feeling roiling inside me from the thrill of it. Swimming to the pontoon, I marvel at the calmness of the water that looks like glass. I wave to Regan when at last I climb the ladder – he waves back. Lying there looking at the sky, I'm soaking in Vitamin D, and a lovely peaceful sensation spreads through me.

I could fall asleep like this.

The calmness is broken when suddenly the whole pontoon starts rocking from side to side. Then it violently shakes, tossing me around like I'm in a tumble dryer, smashing my body against the wood so hard that it's bound to leave bruises. Squirming over, I manage to grasp the rope edging to stabilise myself before I break a bone, or worse.

"Regan, help me!" I yell across the water, but he doesn't hear me, I think he's fallen asleep.

The whole platform tips over, sending me headfirst into the water – it feels like I've smashed my head against a concrete wall. Momentarily stunned, I swallow water as I break through the surface.

"Help, help!" I scream, treading water, but Regan doesn't even flinch.

My head is aching, and everything is turning grey at the edges, as black and white dots spin before my eyes. I come to the realisation that I'm about to drown. Although I'm a competent swimmer, I can't seem to keep my head above the water. Splashing about in a frantic panic only makes the lake more torrential.

Something wet and slimy glides by my legs, giving me a jolt. Then I feel sharp teeth stab into the side of my foot, the pain is excruciating, but I can't scream because I have to hold my breath as we plunge beneath the waves. I know that it can't be a shark or a whale, not in this lake, because it's not connected to the ocean. With my other foot, I boot it hard somewhere on its sludgy and squishy body, it lets go, and so I swim for my life.

I don't dare look back, knowing it's chasing me. The wake of its pursuit forces the currant to swirl around like a whirlpool. I swim faster trying to get away, but it's gaining pace and I'm running out of energy. I feel scales scratch my skin. In pure survival mode, and with all of my remaining strength, I make it to the shore.

As soon as my knees hit the sand, I start puking up filthy black and green liquid. In my peripheral vision, I see Regan sprinting over, while in horror I'm transfixed as I watch my vomit wriggling with hundreds of little translucent worms. It's a challenge to stop myself from throwing up again.

"Ali. What the hell happened?" I hear Regan say, though he sounds like he's miles away, probably because my ears are blocked. All I can hear is the pounding of my heart beating to the beat of a bass drum inside my head. "I was listening to music," he says, taking his EarPods out of his ears. "Is that blood on you?"

My stomach enters my throat, when I look there are small puncture marks on the side of my foot, the flesh is open, and four holes, quite deep, are leaking blood. I take off my T-shirt, hold it over the wound, applying pressure, but it hurts so much I nearly pass out.

“I think I wounded myself when I fell off the platform,” I lie, knowing he isn’t going to believe me about the creature.

I’d made chicken sandwiches, and a cheese and fruit platter for lunch, and we’d bought a bottle of champaign with us to wash it all down, but I can only nibble on a cracker, after what I saw come out of my mouth, it’s well and truly killed my appetite. The bubbly has warmed in the sun, tasting flat and too sweet, making me feel nauseous.

“It’s getting late, can we head back now?” I ask, because I’m starting to shiver in fear and confusion over what just happened. The pain in my foot is so bad it’s practically numbed by the time we make it back to the cabin. The sun is dipping behind the trees, spreading flecks of purple and orange through the heavens.

I stop, in confusion I ask, “Didn’t we lock the door?”

“Yes, so why is the door open?” Regan replies, as astonished as I.

We conduct a sweep of the cabin, but we find no one and nothing seems to be missing.

“Could you boil the kettle please? I’d kill for a coffee. I just have to go to the loo,” I state, trying my best to hide my discomfort.

In the bathroom I realise that my foot is bleeding. Gently I clean the wound and wrap gauze and a bandage around it, that I’d found in the medicine cabinet. Bruises are forming on my body from the knocks I took on the pontoon. I’m about to leave the bathroom, when there are three rapid knocks at the door. I go to open it, but it’s locked, which is odd because the lock is disengaged.

“I can’t open the door. Can you push it open? I think it might be stuck.” Silence replies back. “Regan, open the door,” I shout, trying to pull it open, but it’s no use, it doesn’t budge.

My heart is beating hard, and anxiety frightens me into near hyperventilation. I pound and pound on the door, crying out for Regan.

I'm shocked when the door flies open, hitting the wall. The hallway is empty when I poke my head through the doorway. There's no lock on the other side of the door, so why didn't it open? There's no way anyone could lock me in from this side. But I brush it off and return to the mirror. Looking back at me is a hideous lady, filthy black, like she's covered in muddy water. Her head is bent at an unnatural angle; it's ungodly.

There's a bleeding ring mark around her neck, her eyes as black as the moonless sky, and coming from her mouth is dirty sludge, wriggling with maggots and cockroaches, dropping to the floor.

I run screaming from the bathroom, and almost collide with Regan who is walking out of the kitchen. Attached to his back is the lady from the mirror. I blink and she disappears.

"Where you calling for me?"

"Yes I was! Did you lock me in the bathroom?"

"Don't be ridiculous, I was in here the whole time. Why, what happened?" he asks, looking at my bandage. "What's wrong with your foot?"

"It still aches from when I fell off the pontoon. It had sharp edges, that's all." I hear myself lie again and I have to ask why the hell am I lying to my husband?

As darkness consumes the cabin, and a nighttime chill nestles in, we eat toasted sandwiches and chips in front of the roaring fire.

It's getting late, so I get into bed, where terror plagues my dreams. *I'm running to the lake, laughing and excited as a kid on Christmas day, with Regan running after me holding a dead crab in his hand. He throws it at me and misses as I dive into the lake to escape his prank. The water is dirty brown, and it stinks like sewage, yet I'm happily swimming through it towards the pontoon. Suddenly, an enormous creature that resembles a crocodile, with the body of a dragon without wings, rises through the surface, it's jaws wide open.*

I'm trying to swim faster towards the pontoon and safety, but it's futile. It swallows me in its giant maw of a mouth. Trapped inside with me are hundreds of people, screaming in pain, sobbing in fear, crying in terror.

When Regan falls into bed beside me, I roll away from him. Something inside me has changed since we've arrived here. There's a sense of animosity growing and gnawing away inside me towards my husband, and I don't know why. It's a mystery. Why have my feelings altered so drastically? Is it my gut instincts kicking in? No, it can't be that. I know he'd never hurt me. Or is it some delusional belief that something dreadful is going to happen to me? Am I just being paranoid?

With ruminating thoughts compounding inside my brain, it takes a while but eventually sleep puts me out again. I toss and turn most of the night, coming in and out of dreams, and straight into more nightmares.

It's freezing cold when I wake up. *Why is it so bright in here?* I'm shocked to find myself laid out on the deck, in my PJ's. My face is covered in early morning dew, and the wooden planks wet my back. Sitting up too fast sends the world spinning.

My head hurts, probably from the dive off the pontoon yesterday.

Why the hell am I outside?

After a long hot shower, to take away the chills that are inflicting me with the tremors, I find Regan fast asleep in bed.

"Regan, wake up." I shake his shoulder.

"What, why, oh…morning. I was just having the strangest dream," he says, yawning and glancing at the digital clock. "Why are you up and dressed already? It's only 7 o'clock."

"Something weird happened, I woke up on the deck! Did you put me out there?" I ask, observing him for any deception.

“Why the hell would I do that? Have you lost your mind?”

He looks at me aghast, as if I’ve accused him of murder.

“I don’t know! I was just asking. Perhaps I was sleepwalking?”

“I doubt it, you’ve never done that before. I’ll get up and make us breakfast,” he says, getting off the bed and wrapping me in a hug. He soothes my head with his warm hand, trying to comfort me.

“It’ll be okay. Look, we only have a couple of days left before we head home. Let’s make the most of it. I’ve got some paperwork to finish off, then we’ll go for a walk. Apparently, there’s a waterfall not too far from here. We could have a look, how does that sound?”

“Sounds great.” Though an insidious sense of trepidation succumbs me, after what happened yesterday at the lake. “I’ll go and check my foot again. It was bleeding in the shower.”

I meander off while he gets dressed. I didn't want to tell him what I saw when I was in the shower earlier. My foot has changed colour, it's turning black, and it seems to be spreading. I pop two pain killers dry. *I'm sure I'll be okay.*

When I exit the bathroom the smell of pancakes brightens my mood.

After breakfast, we are getting ready to venture to the waterfall, but I need to check my foot again because now it's aching something fierce.

By the time I reach the bathroom I feel slightly dizzy, like I'm on a boat adrift on a swollen sea. I have to steady myself against the shower. Sitting on the toilet lid, I unwrap the blood-soaked bandage. I nearly vomit when I see that my leg has turned completely black reaching just below the knee. I poke at it with a finger, leaving dents in the skin where I push on it. It's spongy, and green liquid is leaking through a hole. *FUCK!* I know I need to go to the hospital, but if I can wait two more days, then I can go and get help. But then the walk through the bush back to the car will be brutal.

I can't think about that now, I'm not going to let this get in the way. We both really need this time together. If I ruin it, it could mean the end of our marriage. We came here to reconnect.

Back at home things haven't been the best because Regan works too much, and his shifts are too long. While we've been here, I can see he's trying his best to make up for it. Though he still has to pay penance for the stress he caused when I found intimately suggestive texts messages on his cell phone that he'd been sending to a work colleague. He says I took it the wrong way and made it into something more than it was. I don't know for sure if they were seeing each other, as more than just friends, but I have to trust him. He's my husband after all. Though a seething anger slithers through me like a venomous snake, when I think about the messages he'd sent to that skanky bitch, Laura from accounts. I let the thoughts dissolve as I wrap my leg with the last of the bandages. I make a conscious decision there and then to be more grateful towards Regan, since he's doing his best, then I should too.

When I return to the kitchen, Regan is packing the backpack with supplies.

“Are you ready?” he asks, placing a hatchet into the side pocket.

“What’s that for?” I ask, a little taken back.

“Just in case we need to get through the gorse bushes. Why? What do you think it’s for?” A smirk lights his face. He cracks up laughing, but I don’t.

It’s a lovely scenic walk to the waterfall, but my leg is killing me. I don’t complain, although Regan notices and asks, “Why are you limping?”

“It’s just my foot, it’s still a little sore. Nothing to worry about,” I hear the fib, I hope he doesn’t.

The track is steep in places, and managing the incline drains a lot of energy from me. The view from the top of the waterfall is beyond spectacular. The trees go on for miles, lush and green; like the garden of Eden before a snake turned everything rotten. A fine mist sprays us as we look over the edge. The way the sun strokes the water in the pond below is beautiful.

It's an insane one-hundred-foot drop down to the bottom, a slight feeling of vertigo afflicts me, making me back off. One missed step and one would surely meet their maker. The waterfall sounds like a freight train. It's so loud I can't hear anything other than the water. It would be a great remedy for Tinnitus.

We sit on boulders as big as cars, and admire the view, we have to yell above the cacophony.

"It's gorgeous, isn't it darling?" Regan shouts.

"It's stunning. But it's so loud!"

After a while he says he needs to pee and wanders off into the bush. While he's gone, I pull the hatchet from the backpack's pocket. It's heavy in my hands, solid, with a wooden handle, it's brand new, and sparkles in the sun. I hide it behind my back when I see Regan emerge from the bush. He plonks himself beside me. The stink of sweat coming from him flips my stomach. *This was a terrible idea, we should have stayed at the cabin, I could be reading a book in the sun, or suntanning on the deck.* Something feels off, though I don't know what.

Regan's voice breaks me from my daydream. "We could go down and have a swim, it's a warm enough day for it," he suggests.

"Okay darling, let's do that."

He puts the backpack on his shoulders. We start walking, and after a while of descending the track, I suddenly stop. Regan moves on chatting about something I have no interest in. When finally, he notices that I'm not with him, he yells at me to hurry up. That's it, I snap!

It feels like someone has taken over me, is making me do this, and I can't stop the trajectory of horror. I rush at him with the hatchet held high above my head. I stab it into his back, pulling it out, and plunging it back in, over and over until I know for sure he's dead; nearly decapitating him in the chaos. The sound of the blade cutting through flesh and vertebrae is sickening. Clots of blood and matter cloak me, it dribbles down my body, and the ground soaks it up. I push his corpse over the edge, and it drops into the water below with nothing more than an insignificant splash. In shocked disbelief, I see a creature as big as a house swallow him up. Walking back to the cabin, the sun is at my back. I'm tingling with adrenalin, my heart is racing so fast, I think it's about to explode. I can't stop smiling, though all I really want to do is cry.

A week later, after an intensive search of the waterfall, Regan's body still hasn't been located, so it is decided to call off the search. They'll never find him anyway, because the creature took him, but I don't tell them that, no one would believe me anyway. The cops questioned me, but all I could tell them is he slipped from the top of the waterfall, and there was nothing I could do.

My leg is no longer black and green, it's spread to more areas on my body.

It's been a month since Regan died. I'm sitting in the living room when I see a squad car pull up the driveway. I watch his gait as he approaches the front door. He knocks on the door like only a cop does; loud, hard and annoying. After brief introductions, I invite the detective to come inside.

"Are you going somewhere?" he asks, seeing the boxes littered throughout the hallway and the living room.

“Yes, I’m moving away to be closer to my parents. I can’t stand living here without Regan; it breaks my heart.”

He doesn’t know the real reason I’m moving out. I’m trying to get away from Regan. He’s haunting me in my dreams, my nightmares, when I walk into the kitchen, in the car’s rearview mirror, in shop windows, and in bed I can feel his body cold as ice against mine.

“Okay, fair enough,” he comments, breaking me from my reverie. “I’m sorry for your loss. This must be a hard time for you right now, but I’ve come to give you some information you might like to know. The warden at the prison your husband worked for, gave me a call this morning. There’s been a development.”

“Tell me,” I say, twisting my hands into nervous knots.

“The prison is conducting their own investigation, and it would seem your husband wasn’t acting in a professional manner. There are claims he was having relationships with some of the prisoners. He’s also been linked to the death of one of the inmates, she was the owner of the cabin you were staying at. Apparently, it is alleged that your husband was the last person to see her alive. Sorry to have to tell you all of that, but I thought you should know.”

I let it sink in. I ask him, “Do you happen to have a photograph of the owner of the cabin?”

“Yes, I do actually,” he says, scrolling through his cell phone. “Here, this is her. But I can’t disclose her name as it’s an ongoing investigation.”

I take his cell phone, and when I see the photograph, my hand shakes so violently it drops to the carpet.

“Do you recognise her?” he asks, plucking his phone off the floor.

"No. Sorry, I don't," I lie, because I do recognise her, she's the lady in the mirror.

Then I remember the hatchet that Regan packed but didn't use on the way to the waterfall, after all. In hindsight, it seems strange, like I'm missing pieces to the puzzle. What were his real reasons for having it with him that day? Was he going to kill me? Were the ghosts haunting me, trying to warn me that he had sinister intentions? Did he kill the lady in the mirror?

I guess I'll never know.

When the detective leaves, I have an extra hot shower because I feel filthy from the information he dumped on me. When I get out, I wipe the condensation from the mirror. I am shocked frozen to the spot when I look in the glass and see Regan standing behind me. He has the hatchet wedged in his back, and there are bleeding gaping holes where his eyes should be. Beside him is the lady from the cabin, she has a rope wrapped around her neck. It makes me wonder if she'd killed herself, or if her death was meant to look like a suicide, due to the fact she was attached to Regan, I wonder now, is she now attached to me?

Over the next few days, I see Regan and the lady in the mirror everywhere I go. They stand at the foot of my bed, watching me. They lurk in the darkened corners, crawl along the ceiling, drag their broken bodies across the floor. I can't sleep, eat or concentrate. To be honest, I hardly get off the couch anymore. The house is in total disarray, and I spend most of my days flicking through the TV channels. My nails have turned black and are falling off. Bold patches cover my head, pus filled boils lace my face. My body is now covered head to toe in a thick cracking black skin, I can't bear to look at myself, because I have become the lady in the mirror.

Follow Del and her work here:

The Miner's Secret

by Stephen Knight

I hadn't been there for very long. Pontycymer. It was a little village in the South Wales valleys surrounded by history. You could stand at the edge of the lakes just as I had done with my Staffordshire Bull Terrier and imagine the seven hundred black-faced miners tracing up and down the lift shafts of the two mines in the area. Nearly forty years later the prosperity had gone, the village reaped with an air of poverty. The mines had long gone but a lot of the old miners remained. Little did I know that some of them had a secret.

Yes, Stephen Knight was getting away from a messy divorce. I moved to the area because the houses were cheap. Where else does £80,000 get you a three bedroom terraced house with a large garden? It was the garden that started the problems. Overgrown with weeds and bushes, it was my first task. I paid for the assistance of a young sixteen year old boy whose mother had told me that he was struggling to find work. With what little dry days experienced in the village we managed to move the earth, pile up and burn the weeds and the roots of dead trees and then shape the garden.

I was aching. "We will finish soon, Rhys," I shouted over to the boy. "Looks like it is going to rain in any case," I continued as I looked up to the grey sky hanging over us.

"That's a good idea, Steve," he replied as he put down the shovel that he was using to scoop up the large red bricks that had buried themselves beneath the soil.

Before I knew it, the time had flown, and I was in bed. That is when the first of the unusual experiences started. I was dozing off, head heavy in my memory foam pillow when suddenly there was a tapping on what sounded like was coming from the back door. I thought that tricks were playing with my mind at first. Perhaps I was overtired. But as I sat up and listened, I realised that I wasn't going out of my mind. There was breathing, heavy breaths, coming from a baritone voice. Was there someone in my house? The tapping was becoming more prominent as I made my way onto the landing and then walked down the stairs. Was my welcome to the village going to be one of the feral youths who I have been warned about, waiting for me downstairs to rob me of what little I had left when the wife and I had parted company?

Someone was definitely there. Downstairs. As I reached the dividing door from the kitchen to the side extension, everything stopped. No breathing. No noise. Just silence. I looked at my watch. 23:20 hrs.

The next day was rest day. I thought that I would get out and about and get my face known, and in any case Rhys could not help me as he had other appointments. The local café beckoned.

“Hello. Could I have a bacon roll and a latte, please?” I asked the elderly assistant who looked like she had been there years what with her greasy apron wrapped around her waist and the greetings to other customers before me, all of whom she was on first name terms.

“£4.50,” she replied as she turned and started frying the bacon in the pan. “Haven’t seen you around here before,” she exclaimed as she looked at me and then back at the bacon.

“No,” I replied as I took a seat at the table not far from the counter. “I’ve just moved into the Avenue.”

"Good luck," she said sarcastically. "What number?"

Why she wanted to know that was beyond me. I had visions of her knocking on the door for a night of passion, taking the conversation we were having as an invite to come around for more than coffee. "Sixty-six."

She stopped everything that she was doing. "Sixty-six?" she enquired with widened eyes. She looked scarier than I felt.

"Yes. Why?"

"Nothing. No. Don't worry about it," she said as she suddenly carried on with her cooking.

"Is anything wrong with it?"

She took the pan away from the burner. "Look. I don't want to be the bearer of bad news. But. Well. Just be careful, okay?"

“Why?” I enquired with the thoughts of what had happened the previous night now solidifying in my head. “Is there something wrong?”

The big man stood in the doorway. He looked like a regular customer as his frame filled that of the doorway. His face red as though the walk from his car to the café had taken its toll on him. It was obvious that his food was more important than his health. “She will say no more! I don’t want her scaring you,” he exclaimed as his face stared at her. I could see that the woman was frightened, a change in her demeanour instantaneous with the man’s presence in the café.

That was the end of all my conversation in that place. I knew that I would never return.

My house started to feel cold at all times of the day and night. As I breathed, the mist from the exhaling air made it feel like it was freezing outside even though it wasn’t. It was only afternoon. Already I could hear the tapping on the back door. I looked through the partition window. There was no one there. I began to wonder if it were a branch from a tree or something blowing onto the extension. Was I imagining things?

“BANG!” It made me jump. I was sat down reading a book at the time.

“What the hell?” I bellowed out as I realised that there was a noise upstairs. This time I wasn’t afraid but inquisitive. I dropped my book onto the sofa and jumped up, walked to the stairs and started ascending slowly. Okay, so I may have been a little scared. As I reached the top my head turned from side to side. All the doors were open, exactly as I had left them, apart from one, the spare bedroom. It looked like it had slammed shut. Easily done, I thought to myself. Wind from outside had obviously blown in through the window. The open window. I walked over and tried the door handle. The door was sealed as though it had been locked from the inside. But there were no locks, I thought to myself. Maybe it had just jammed when it had slammed shut so loudly. I used my shoulder to try and force it open. It wouldn’t budge. Perhaps the mechanism inside the door handle had broken. I forced it down as far as it would go and then with all my strength, shouldered the door several times. It opened unexpectedly and I fell forward onto the ground. “Shit!” As I laid their slightly shaken by my fall I looked up to the window. The closed window.

“BANG! BANG! BANG!”

Quickly I got up and brushed myself down. “What now?” I asked myself as I walked back out into the darkened upstairs hallway. The remaining three doors; the main bedroom, the storage room and the bathroom, had all slammed shut just like their predecessor. I felt the blood leave my body. I was as cold as the house itself. The hairs on the back of my neck were standing up. “Oh my God,” I said to myself. The thoughts were going through my mind. Had I bought a haunted house? It was now scaring me. I didn’t want to admit it to myself, but if the house was haunted, at that moment in time who or whatever was doing the haunting was winning. I went to go back down the stairs telling myself that if the ghost wanted the doors shut then so be it. I wasn’t going to argue. I quickly went back downstairs and picked up the book. That tapping on the back door was still there.

Sunday morning. I wasn’t one for going to church but on this occasion I felt the need to do just that. Perhaps the local priest could shed some light on the strange goings on at 66 The Avenue. I dressed up quite smartly and headed down to St David’s church at the other end of the Avenue, so not far.

There was general chit-chat amongst the parishioners. I was the stranger in the midst. The place went quiet. I thought that only happened in pubs, like it did in '*The Slaughtered Lamb'* in the movie *'An American Werewolf in London.'* I felt the coldness, not because a lack of heat but a lack of welcome, an atmosphere that you could cut with a knife. No one welcomed me. All eyes were on me until the church organ started and everyone sat down. I sat on my own at the back. It was like that for the hour.

The vicar of St Davids was stood at the door at the end of the service saying goodbye to everyone. He was an older man, someone who looked like he had seen a lot of life. I stood at the back of the queue waiting to say my farewells. I overheard his *'Nice to see you again, thank you for coming,'* to the person in front of me. His facial expression changed as he looked at me, and I wasn't sure if it was through guilt or fear that he started to look around, including at some of the congregation that had decided to gather outside of the main door. "Father, I need to speak to you about something." He stared at me, continuing to look to and fro from me and the crowd outside. He tapped my hand.

"Thank you for coming. It will have to be later, my son."

Not even the priest of the local parish would speak to me, I thought to myself as I left. The locals were still gathering outside, turning their heads and staring as I walked past. It was frightening to think that something like this still occurred in the 21st century. I went back home, closed the door behind me and made sure it was locked and secured by the additional bolts. I found myself checking all the windows and the rear door. I was safe. Well, sort of.

I would have never expected a knock at the door at 22:35 hours. I looked out of the living room window, questioning myself whether it could just be an addition to the tapping at the back door that was now a regular occurrence. It was the priest. Did he had time to speak to me at this time of the evening?

"Hello, Father," I said apprehensively as I opened the door. He didn't stand around but pushed himself into my hallway, looking behind him suspiciously as he did. I closed the door.

“I haven’t got long,” he exclaimed nervously. “I cannot stay.”

“Why?” I asked inquisitively. “What is wrong with this place?”

“It has secrets. There is a strange presence here!” He said as his face started to go bright red, and it looked like he was gasping for breath as though someone or something was strangling him. Suddenly there was a loud screaming coming from upstairs.

“What the…?” I questioned as I turned to look up the stairs. I felt drained and cold, and my eyes widened at the sound.

“I’ve got to go. The presence is attacking me. He doesn’t want me here!” He quickly brushed past me, reopened the door and stepped back outside. “Check the newspapers! Check the newspapers!”

The screaming stopped as soon as I closed the door. It was the quickest visit I had even had from someone. It threw me totally. I wasn't sure who was more frightened, me or the priest. I froze, my feet stuck to the floor, my eyes staring to the first floor landing. But at last I had the start of my answers to what was happening.

The night was quite frantic. The tapping on the back door and the sound of heavy breathing continued. The fact that I had wedged all the doors open with rubber stoppers didn't stop them slamming constantly. I didn't sleep. I couldn't. Those last words of the priest were echoing in my mind. 'Check the newspapers.' Normally I would have just googled it, but, I know it sounds funny, but I didn't want the entity knowing what I was doing. Yes, I was that frightened.

When the daylight filled the sky, I walked down to the bus stop, paranoia settling in to check if I was being followed and then questioning myself as to whether I was just being stupid. I caught the number 72 bus into Bridgend Town. After figuring out where their library was, I made my way there for the first part of my investigation.

The records were so old. At first I googled *'Ghost Pontycymer'* which brought up incomplete information dating back to the 1970's. There were no computer records back then, I told myself. Not unless they had transferred them all over which, with a paper as small as the South Wales Gazette, was very unlikely. So it was down to good old fashioned microfiche. It took me three days and a whole lot of bags under my eyes before I found something. I scrolled through the records of the newspaper firstly recorded on 27th April 1978.

'Pontycymer man missing.'

Police are looking for a 52 year old man who has been missing for three days. Rhydian Williams of the Avenue, Pontycymer was last seen at St David's Church in the village on the morning of 23rd April. He is said to be approx. 5'10", well built and at the time of his disappearance was wearing a black suit, white shirt and red tie. Anyone with information please contact Pontycymer Police station.

The following days showed stories with pleads from his wife, Rhian, and his sixteen-year-old son David. There was more to this that met the eye I was sure of it. One thing I had to do was make peace with Rhydian. I went home on my third day of research. The tapping was still on the back door, tap-tap-tap. The heavy breathing ringing around in my head. On the window sill in the living room I had placed my small collection of crystal paperweights. As I stood there, one of the paperweights flung across the room. I ducked down and it smashed on the wall behind me. That was it.

"RHYDIAN! STOP! PLEASE STOP! I KNOW WHO YOU ARE!" The second of the paperweights flew at my head this time and missed me by a few inches. The doors upstairs slammed and continued slamming as though they were being opened and slammed shut over and over again. "WHAT DO YOU WANT?" I demanded to know. The third paperweight came my way, this time it hit me centre chest and winded me. I crouched forward and tried to catch my breath, then forward onto my knees. I felt I may be safer down low. I recovered slowly. "I AM NOT AFRAID OF YOU! COME ON! GIVE ME YOUR BEST SHOT!"

The doors stopped banging. The thought went through my mind of him being tired out. He could have been, after all, in reality nearly a hundred years old. In a less angry voice, I said, “I want to help you. You are obviously angry at something or someone. Tell me what you want! Please!” Everything went quiet. The tapping on the door stopped. The heavy breathing ceased. For the first night since I had been in my new house, I managed to get a good night’s sleep until the next morning. I tried to move my body. I was lying on my back in my bed. I couldn’t move. It felt like something was holding me down, something strong. I managed to turn my head to either side but that was it. With what strength I could muster I was trying to push my arms up and kick my legs, but they were pinned. It felt like there was a hand around my throat. I couldn’t breathe. It stopped. I gasped out loudly.

One thing that had been on my mind was the knowledge that Pastor Martin Jones had about checking the newspapers. He was old enough to have been in the area for decades, exactly how long that Rhydian had been missing. Did he know something more? Why was the entity of Rhydian Williams attacking him and not allowing him in his old home?

I walked down to the church and copied down the telephone number that was on the noticeboard outside. If Father Jones couldn't see me at my house, perhaps I could see him at his. It was arranged. 14:00 hrs this afternoon at the church. The priest told me that he felt safer discussing Rhydian Williams within the presence of the Lord at the church.

The time came around and I had taken a stroll down to the church. It was a simple building, red brick with no thought into the design. I walked up the steps and the door was open and so I walked in. There was no one around and so I called out, "Hello. Father?"

Suddenly at the back of the church next to the pulpit the man appeared. "Hello. I'm here," he said as he walked forward. He wasn't alone. I saw a shadow of a second man behind him who finally come into the dim light from the burning candles on the side. "Can I introduce David Williams."

"We've met," I answered negatively as I saw the man from the café.

“We meet again,” the man exclaimed as he held out his hand for me to shake. I guessed who he was from the name, but I didn’t want him to know that I knew, well, not at this point. Let them tell me.

“Come, sit down,” Father Jones said as he pointed to the pew on the left. The three of us did just that.

“I’ve been told that you have moved into my old house. I lived there with my parents when I was growing up,” David said quite openly.

“Yes. That’s right,” I responded whilst showing an element of fear in my voice. “Although I’m not having a good time there at the moment.”

“I have to tell you.“ The vicar said as he gave David a sly look, “The house has an entity. It is known to be haunted. Many have lived there. Many have left. The house has been empty for a long while.”

“Do you know who or what is haunting it? I mean, why are you here David? Is it something to do with you?” I looked at the man who was sat further away on the other side of the priest. “And why was this ‘entity’ attacking a man of the cloth, Father? I thought it was going to kill you.”

The pair looked at each other as there was a momentary silence and then Father Jones nodded to David. “We think it is the ghost of my Dad. He disappeared in 1978. Not a trace. The Police couldn’t track him down.”

“So why would he haunt the house?”

David was acting guiltily. His face was all void and red and he kept looking into the eyes of the vicar. “We don’t know,” he said sheepishly. “It is only since his death that the hauntings have been happening.”

My head filled with a frown. Why was my ghost's son talking about his death in 1978? He had just disappeared in 1978. They didn't know that he had, in fact, died at all in that year. Yet David was here saying such things and the priest was backing him up with nods of the head at everything he was saying. "Doesn't he want anyone in his house or something?"

"Quite possibly," the priest said softly. "He was very much a private man."

"So you knew him?" I asked.

"I was born and bred in Pontycymer. David and I grew up together. Went to the same school. We even worked down the mine together with Rhydian."

"Well. Your Father is going to have to get used to me being there, David. I'm not budging, no matter how violent he is. I'm doing up the house as we speak, starting with the garden."

There was suddenly an atmosphere that you could cut with a knife. Both men were silent until David looked at me with worried eyes. “The…the. G…arden,” he stuttered.

“Yes. I am landscaping it. The plan is to have it looking better than it is right now.”

The lies came thick and fast. I could tell it. Something was wrong. They seemed to have a secret between them. Had I hit the nail on the head? The priest perked up. “That is when the other residents who have tried to live there have had problems. When they have tried to do something to the garden,” he snapped.

“Dad loved his garden,” David added quickly. “He had flowers everywhere. Perhaps if you leave it as it is, the haunting may stop.”

“Really,” I answered unconvincingly.

“In fact, I must ask you to stop. As a memory of my Dad,” David continued.

I nodded. Something was definitely wrong. I chose to play along with his request. There was a relevance in my investigation. The garden had hit a nerve with the pair. “Okay. Maybe just a tidy up, then. Cut the weeds back.” David nodded and again there was a silence. I noticed the pair look at each other again. “Well I had better get back to my haunted house.” I got up. “Just that still doesn’t answer my question on why this ‘entity’ doesn’t like you, Father? I was going to ask you to come around and bless the place.”

“It may be best that I get my colleague from the church in Bettws. He may have better success. I can arrange that if you so wish?”

“Please. It may help, who knows.” I looked at the pair. There was still an uneasy feeling there. “I’ll see you soon. Thank you for the information.” I left with a sense of suspicion. They had guilt written all over their faces. I walked home. Time to do some gardening, I thought to myself.

Thursday soon dawned. Young Rhys turned up, desperate to earn some much needed pocket money in order that he could join his friends in going out on the town.

“What are we doing today,” he asked as he tried to work out which tools to take up from the extension to the garden.

I looked at him. “I hope your muscles are good,” I said to him. “Today we start to dig, remove some of the roots of the dead trees and begin landscaping.” I laughed at the expression on his face. “I might treat you to a beer afterwards.”

“I hope it’s more than one,” he said as he looked at the amount of work that still had to be done.

Three hours passed. I’m not sure what type of tree that it used to be. It looked like it had been cut down some time ago. I drilled several holes in the wood and poured accelerant into them and then lit it. The stump would need to be burnt out to a certain extent. “Come back tomorrow,” I said to the boy. “This should be done by then.” Rhys jumped over the back gate to save going through the house and having to remove his muddy shoes.

I watched him walk up the lane. But suddenly there was a familiar face stood looking over the fence.

“How’s it going?” David Williams stood there, staring at my garden work.

“Checking up on me?” I asked. “You know, if I didn’t know better, I would say that you have a bit of a guilt complex. Is there something that you want to tell me?” I asked jokingly whilst trying to portray a sense of humour in what I was saying.

He didn’t take it very well. “I thought we had agreed about the garden. What with the fire?”

I could see the look of horror in his face. “Just burning out all the old tree stumps. We will pull them out tomorrow.”

David nodded. “Well if you need a hand, I can come down.”

“The more the merrier. Tomorrow. 10:00am. You can help me get this lump out then.” He walked off.

For once the house didn't feel cold. It was like the man I was sharing the house with knew something that I didn't. There was no disturbances through the night. It was all quiet on the western front. I was glad because I was aching all over after the gardening and just needed sleep.

The next morning, true to his word, David Williams arrived in his car and parked in the space that was available at the end of the garden. I looked and saw Father Martin Jones in tow sat in the passenger seat.

Rhys looked up the garden. "Brilliant!" he said excitedly. "Extra hands!"

"Here," David said nervously as he carried a rope down towards the tree stump. "We can use the car to pull it out. Save your energy." He watched Martin head down with a spade in his hands.

"I can help you fill in the hole afterwards," he said. "I have my trusted spade and fork."

I let them get on with it, watching as David wrapped the rope around the stump and secure it before heading back to his car. “Okay,” I shouted as I pushed Rhys away from the scene. David waved and then began reversing. The wheels skidded on the uneven surface of the lane as it was riddled with loose stones but gradually the tree started to move. Both the vicar and I assisted in the removal by using our spades to cut through any remaining roots. With one last rev of the engine the stump flew backwards and up towards the back of the garden.

“Arrggghhhhh!” Martin shouted as he lost his footing. I tried to catch him but was too late as he fell forwards into the huge excavation which looked like it was some ten to twelve feet deep. He became frantic. He started panicking. He started screaming out loud. “No! No! Arrghhhh! Arrghhh!”

“It’s okay, Martin. I’ll get you ou…” I froze as I looked down into the pit. The vicar was laid on top of bones. As he panicked a little more I could see a skull, then the hands and the feet.

“It’s him! It’s him!”

David Williams rushed down to the hole and looked in, then looked at me and screamed, “I told you not to interfere! Leave things as they are! But no!”

Rhys saw the dangers and was on his mobile and calling the emergency services.

“Hang up! NOW!” David demanded. “Otherwise, you will be joining him,” he exclaimed as he pointed down to the priest.

I looked down once more. Father Jones was struggling to breathe. He was face down, his head looking directly at the skull. “Ah. Ah,” he said before continuing in a soft painful voice, “He…l…p me.”

“Shit! He’s having a heart attack!” I said but realised that it was too dangerous to climb down after him. The mud from the hole was already starting to cave in on top of him.

David, on the other hand jumped down to help Martin. “Get the rope! Get the rope!” He said as he looked up. It was too late. The large pile of earth, weeds, brambles, rocks and red bricks that Rhys and I had dug for the past week suddenly caved in on top of both men.

“Shit! Shit!” I said as I fell backwards to escape the possibility of getting dragged in myself. “Rhys! Call the Police! Fire brigade! Ambulance! Anyone!”

It was too late. The emergency services arrived. We dug. David Williams and Martin Jones had been crushed under all the landslide of the garden. The Police forensic teams excavated the pair together with the skeleton. Something told me I had found Rhydian Williams.

The evening soon came around. I sat quietly in the living room as the excavation in the back garden continued. The doors upstairs all banged once. I looked over to the doorway leading to the bottom of the stairs. It didn’t scare me. There was a man, faint with an ethereal glow, the light from behind him shimmering. It was a miner, all dressed in black, tattered clothes, blackened eyes from the coal dust.

It was cold again. I could feel his presence, but it wasn't threatening. Suddenly two further apparitions appeared. One appeared to be threatening the miner. I watched in horror. It was like I wanted to stand up and help him. One of the ghosts swung viciously at the darkened figure that I had first seen with what looked like a small pick axe. The helpless miner fell to the floor. I saw the faces of the two behind him. David had killed his Father. The vicar had assisted him.

Suddenly there was a screaming from the two as cloaked, faceless figures brushed past me and through me giving me the feeling that I was alive, it felt like I had survived an electric shock as I gasped. The two criminals were engulfed as the black figures wrapped themselves around them. Their bodies appeared to be torn apart although all that was left was particles of air. They had gone.

Rhydian Williams had been freed. He had shown me what had happened to him. Why? I will never know why his own son and his best friend had killed the miner. His own Father in David's case. The black figure rose, pointed at me and nodded.

That was the last time that there was any paranormal activity in 66, The Avenue, Pontycymer. In the garden, the flowers bloom like no other. One of my roses is named the Rhydian rose. I hope he likes it.

RIP Rhydian Williams. Born 15/04/1942. Murdered 27/04/1978.

Follow Stephen and his work here:

Contact

by John Dodd

“We’re not the first ones who made it out here then?” Jackson looks on the scanner at the massive number of ships that landed around the temple.

“No one’s claimed right of contact yet,” I glance down at the readings, “And all those ships are deactivated, no batteries, no reactor signs, no life signs.”

“No life signs we can see,” Jackson shakes his head and paces back over, “Some of those ships are this year’s model, no way they’d be out of power.”

“You shall come without need to return,” I quote the message as it had been broadcast out to all the known worlds, “You will come to learn the truth of an elder civilisation and be grateful that you did.”

“Yeah, look, I’m in this for the contact bonus,” Jackson taps the screen, “I’m not here to convert to some weird faith and spend the rest of my life praying in a mouldy temple.”

"We'll get it, fear not..." I turn the ship and head south towards the planet's equator, marking the course as I go, "There's too much foliage in the area for us to land anywhere near, probably the same thought all of them had, we'll get some clear space and trek in from there."

"We don't need to be taking trophies then?" Raptor hangs his necklace in the locker, then turns to check the action on his rifle.

"You of all people don't need to speak of trophies," I nod to him.

"This?" He glances down at the missing little finger on his left hand with a grin, "Told you, that was payment for a debt back in my youth."

"As opposed to a mistake made by kids playing with axes..." I smirk.

"Well, the other kid was Japanese," His grin gets broader, "and his dad had a tattoo, sounds better than getting your hand stuck in a tree."

“Yeah, well, making first contact should be done by us, not our bullets,” I check the rounds in my own gun before sliding it into the holster, “We’re only taking these in case the others who’ve landed had the same idea.”

“What do we need to do then?” Raptor frowns as he slings his rifle over his shoulder and takes a bandolier of grenades from the locker.

“First contact, right?” Jackson looks over in bemusement, “First contact with grenades is called *an invasion*.”

“Any race capable of sending out a signal that reached over three galaxies in every language ever, is more than capable of talking to us,” I check the data on the tablet, “All we’ve got to do is go there, speak to them, establish if they’re friendly or not, and then leave and collect the fat bounty…”

“Uh huh…” Raptors grunt signals his disbelief, “And we’re here for the bounty, which means that anyone else who’s already made contact will be happy to drop us so they keep it.”

"Maybe," I lock my helmet into place and check the air supply, "But that's why we get paid the big bucks."

The lights go out as the ship touches down, the cabin dark, no emergency lighting at all.

Raptor flicks his torch on, "Told you we should get a real engineer." He grins over at Jackson as the mechanic pulls his tools out of his locker.

"Guess I'm staying here for a while then," Jackson sighs, making his way past us, "Don't have too much fun with the aliens, y'hear?"

"I'll save you some," Raptor's grin turns feral, "As long as they don't taste like beef."

"I'm never going to ask how you know these things," Jackson smiles as he heads down the stairs to the engineering bay.

"Come on," I check the map on the tablet, "We get moving now and he'll have this ready for when we get back."

Winding the steps down manually takes twenty minutes, I'm never going to tell Jackson he can't have spare parts ever again. The atmosphere outside is breathable, comparable levels of elements to earth, certainly less harmful than the ship scrubbed air we're used to breathing, but I don't take the helmet off as we make our way through the thick foliage.

"Shit..." Raptor pauses from hacking through the trees with his energy blade, "Couldn't you have found us a route that had a road on it?"

"Every road was full of vehicles, every open space full of spacecraft," I look around, the suits sensors showing life everywhere, insects, birds, all of them are things it hasn't got in its database. "This was the shortest route."

"Great," He hands me the blade, "Lead on.

It's early evening by the time the temple comes into view, a journey that should have taken us two hours on a straight march lengthened to more than five hours of hard hacking and scrambling. I pause at the top of the hill, sitting on a rock and looking down at the starship graveyard surrounding the temple.

"Anyone we know down there?" I look over at Raptor.

"That big one belongs to the Karsi faction from the Jovian imperialists," He sits next to me, "Forty people just to get that in the air, much less come out scouting."

"And yet no power signs," I look around, "And no noise…"

"Not even animals," Raptor nods, switching his suit over to recharge and retracting his helmet into the shoulder guards with a shrug, "Been breathing heavier with all the hacking we've been doing, don't have enough air to get back to the ship as is, and the readings here are showing as clean as anything I've ever breathed."

I nod, my own helmet following suit as I retract the polymer, the air is thick, like breathing soup with the weight of oxygen in it. I take a deep breath and look down again. “Do you want to go down now or do we wait for the morning?”

“Dunno about you boss,” He leans against the rocky outcrop, “I’m beat, if we have to go in there and potentially face off against the others that are looking, I’d rather at least be rested.”

“Alright, set the perimeter, I’ll send word back to Jackson.” I switch the comms over to long range and listen to the static, “Miro to Jackson.”

Static

“Miro to Jackson, come in,” I try again.

Static

“We’re not too far out,” Raptor looks up from where he’s setting the sensors, “Must be the same interference we’re getting on the scanners.”

“I’ll send a drone,” I take the small rotorcraft from my backplate and switch it to record, “Jackson, this is Miro, at the temple site now, going in tomorrow, if you don’t hear from us in twenty four hours, come get us.”

The drone flies up and is gone from sight in less than a minute. I lean back against the rock as Raptor finishes laying the last of the sensors.

“Anything comes within thirty metres of here, we’ll know about it.” He takes his pack from his back plate and passes me a ration pack, “I’ll take first watch…”

The night passes without incident, but the lack of any animal noise is disquieting to say the least. I wake Raptor as the morning sun rises up over the valley.

“Anything?” He looks around at the sensors.

“Not a thing,” I stand, looking down at the tablet, “Come on, there’s something wrong with this picture.”

“Could have told you that from the first second we stepped out of the ship,” He stands and checks through his gear, loading the sensors up and taking his rifle out, “Alright, lead on.”

The temple is old stone, built from the sweat of slaves in times when vengeful gods offered their words through selfish men. The air down in the valley is cooler, a faint smell of stone and copper in the air as we move towards the main entrance.

“Hundreds of footprints,” Raptor crouches down to look at the mud surrounding the entrance, “But all of them going in, none of them coming out.”

“Anything inside?”

He shoulders the rifle and pulls out his motion scanner, sweeping it over the entrance, “Just you and me, you sure about this, boss?”

“One hour,” I take a deep breath, “I don’t like this any more than you do.”

Raptor nods and clips his scanner to his rifle, moving into the dark silence. I follow close behind, the tablet showing the transcription of the message in the mid gloom. I look around the cut stone walls, no moisture, no signs of wear on them, but it's as cold as the mountains around us. There's a faint smell of ozone in the air, a faint breeze from deeper inside the temple, another smell, almost familiar. Raptor looks back at me and taps his nose before continuing onwards. The stone corridor continues on for more than a hundred feet, opening out into a vast, well lit chamber, dry stone walkways as far as the eye can see. I look around, it's not a chamber…

It's a library…

Bookshelves line the stone walls, each of them loaded with thick tomes of leather and paper. I clip the tablet to my arm and motion for Raptor to keep an eye out as I take one of the books from the shelves. It's written in a language I don't understand, all glyphs and symbols, the ink is a dark red with a strange smell to it. The pages are thick and heavy, the whole book no more than twenty pages long. I place it on the nearby lectern and run the tablet over it.

A biography, the life and times of Argrath Veris, Entrepreneur and Explorer. It's written in Seris, the native tongue of the Chern, and Chern sounds like flesh being shredded by metal, so I just read the words. I set the tablet to analyse the ink on the page and read what I can of the translation. Veris was a Chern who specialised in ancient artefacts and relics. He came here to find the elders and then chose to remain behind. The tablet chimes as the analysis completes and it shows up the results.

Blood, Human Blood.

I look around the room as a chill creeps up my spine. "Raptor," I whisper.

"Boss," He turns back for a second, then paces towards me, keeping his rifle trained on the room.

"Written in human blood," I gesture to the book.

"That's enough for me," He glances to the hundreds of thousands of books lining the walls, "Let's get out of here."

I put the first book back, and take a second, placing it on the lectern. The pages are written in Imperial, but the ink is green with purple streaks throughout it and the words look like they were written by a child. I set the tablet analysing the ink and start to read.

Another biography, Emilia Inikova, Explorer and Warrior from the martian colonies, came to the elders for wisdom, chose to remain behind…

The tablet chimes, this ink is also blood, Ratlin blood.

I frown and close the book, placing it back on the shelf and taking another one.

Three books later, I'm getting the picture, all of the books are records of a persons deeds, they came for whatever they came for, then chose to stay with the elders for reasons that are never discussed. Always written in the blood of a creature not the same species as them.

“We should get out of here,” Raptor glances over as I close the last book, “Before we start thinking it’s a good idea to stay behind.”

“We need to find out what’s behind all this,” I put the book back on the shelf and look at him, “In here must be something that we can use.”

“Sure they felt that as well,” He looks down at the books.

“Come on, it’s not like they wrote it in their own blood,” I look around the room in wonder, “And how many books are here, if they’re all like this, this must have been around forever.”

“Then it’ll be here when we come back with more people,” Raptor is insistent, “Come on, we can be back at the ship before the sun goes down.”

“Just a while longer,” I move forwards into the library, looking up at the shelves stretching down into infinity, there are two glass boxes mounted on railings at the side of the room, a small door leading to each from the chamber. “Elevators?” I look at Raptor.

“Don’t know,” He looks spooked now.

“What do you think?”

“I think we need to get out of here, I may not be a cat, but I’m pretty sure curiosity is nearby…” He moves over, pressing the button on the wall and waiting as the door slides open, then leaning in and looking around. “Buttons, hence elevator.”

“To where though…?” I look in and around the box.

“Seriously?” He steps into the elevator and gestures to the buttons on the side, “It’s an elevator, it goes up, it goes down, come on boss…”

I straighten up and nod, “Alright, we’re…”

The doors to the box hiss closed and the box disappears into the darkness below as if dropped.

“Raptor,” I thumb my comms, “Raptor.”

“I’m here,” I can hear the sound of the elevator around his voice, “Wait there, I’m not staying down here, I’ll be back up soon.”

“Alright,” I look around the chamber, “Right here, level…” I look at the symbol by the lift, “Squiggle, Dog, House.”

“Yep, I see it, wait there…”

I wait in oppressive silence, a minute, two, I thumb my comms again.

“Raptor?”

Silence…

“Raptor?”

“I’m here,” His voice sounds distorted, “Elevators not coming back up, stay the fuck where you are and keep an eye out, it’s a charnel house down here.”

"Alright," I move into the middle of the library, looking at the platform in the middle of the room where a table and throne are placed, above it a rack of books and a series of stone arms carved around the throne, four bridges of carved black obsidian leading to it. "Get back up here, we're gone."

I walk around to the nearest bridge, taking a careful step on it and making my way over to the middle.

Safer where I can see everything…

I look at the throne, at the writing all around it, taking my tablet out and scanning the words in. A sound like scuttling from behind me and I spin around, the movement nearly overbalancing me off the side. I sit down on the side of the table, looking at the wall of books where the noise came from.

Nothing…

I look up at the pillar above the throne, a thousand arms and hands carved on all sides of them, all shapes and sizes, some human, some insect, some…

I have no ideas what that is…

The tablet chimes and I pick it up in trembling hands, looking at the translation.

Life, in return for immortality, those who sit upon me will live forever with the elders, their legacy preserved for all time.

I search for artefacts similar to this one, to references in other cultures and times, to anything that might have some knowledge of this.

Nothing…

It's more than an hour before Raptor makes it all the way back up to the level I'm on, he paces slowly over to me, not saying a word till he's close to me.

“Gods of Karna,” He sighs, leaning heavily on the table, “Bodies, thousands of them, the ground floor is littered with them, and the stairs all the way up have got bits of them from where they fell. All of them have still got their equipment on them, but they look like they’ve been dumped there, no one’s come looting.”

“Didn’t think to grab any trophies?” I try to lighten the mood.

“What,” He makes a weary grin, “And have you sitting here shitting it till I got back?”

“Been doing that anyway,” I grin, “Come on, we’re out of here.”

“Alright,” He levers himself off the desk and legs weary from a thousand steps fail under him, causing him to sit on the throne.

His posture changes as he makes contact with the throne, his whole demeanour changing as he looks down at his hands in confusion, then up at me. His mouth opens and his vocal chords clench around a sound that a human cannot pronounce. He stares at me and tries to speak again, then nods, laying back in the throne as the stone arms above move and place a book on the table in front of him.

He sags in the chair as the stone arms move over the book, opening it to the first page and bringing down an index finger as the first drop of red emerges from the end of it. I move forwards to try and pull Raptor out of the chair and his arm comes up, the movement stilted, as if not familiar with moving limbs shaped like that.

“No,” The words are thick, the accent not his, not any humans, “Back.”

I step back, watching as the stone hand writes lines of thick red in the book, the language isn’t English, nor Zuni.

And he doesn’t know any other languages.

I watch in silence as the hand writes page after page in deep red, unable to tear myself away from the sight. The hands stop and then reach forwards to close the book, transferring it up the structure of hands to the empty shelves of the library far above. I look back down at Raptor, his eyes dull, his face slack, nothing remaining of the man who came in with me. The stone hands reach down and pull his body upwards into the other hands, this time moving the body over to the empty space between the bridges.

They release…

The body falls from sight without a word, and the sound of cracking stone echoes above me, I look up as a new pair of arms emerge from the stone high above. Powerful, muscular arms, the left hand missing its little finger…

I run back across the bridge and to the stone corridor, out into the oppressive heat of the jungle and back along the trail that we cut yesterday, much of it already regrowing. It's more than five hours of half running, half stumbling before I make it back to the ship.

The ramp is still down and the power still off. I run up the ramp and gag at the sight before me.

Jackson never fixed the ship…

What's left of him is scattered over three consoles, the wiring has been torn out by uncaring teeth, and the footprints in his blood lead further into the ship, not back down the stairs. Still gasping for air, I turn and run back to the temple with the sound of skittering creatures all around me.

As I reach the perimeter, I look back as the skittering ceases and see the small yellow eyes of a hundred tiny predators staring back at me. They don't move forwards, the line where the trees stop growing is the line they don't pass.

They know it's not safe in there…

I lay on the ground and wait for my heart to stop trying to burst out of my chest, drawing in ragged breaths of thick air as the creatures pace back and forth, each of them keeping those tiny eyes upon me, none of them willing to breach the barrier.

I climb up on the high stone surface at the front of the temple where they couldn't follow and sleep fitfully till the mornings light. Looking down at the jungle, I can see that the ferns and trees are still moving, often like a wave, as if a herd of tiny creatures were moving as one.

Can't go back that way.

I look at the supplies in my pack, food enough for three days if I stretch the rations, water enough for two.

The ship is a half day away and I don't know how to fix it…

I pull the tablet out and take a look at the data it gathered, each of the books I scanned shows the person who wrote it *chose* to stay with the elders.

Choice is sometimes a lack of options…

I spend another day on the warm stone, trying to think of another way, some possible chance of getting out of this, then I think back to the thousands of books in the library, most of them would have stood where I am now, and if they couldn't…

On the fifth day, hungry beyond reckoning and all but dehydrated, I stumble back into the library, looking up at the throne, taking my tablet and leaving it on the table before taking a deep breath.

Better to live somehow than to die like this…

I sit…

I look through a hundred eyes as the body on the throne looks in shock at the hands, then nods as the stone arms bring another book down and start to write in it. Faintly I hear voices in the ether, a convocation of minds, unburdened by the needs of the body. The words in other languages, but I understand their meaning, I understand their purpose. I try to speak and hear my own voice in the void, others answering, welcoming me.

Time ceases to have meaning, there are only the others, there are only the words, a million different creatures from a thousand different worlds, all united in common purpose. I speak until I have no words left to give, I listen till the words no longer make sense to me and I know that it is time.

I open my eyes to find myself upon the throne again, looking down at the scything claws that are now my arms. Another mantis like creature leans in towards me and I raise a claw to stop it from coming closer, looking up as the book that will remember me is laid in front of me. I see the stone hand moving to the page and know what I want to say.

My name is Miro, explorer and hunter of treasure, I came here to find wealth, I was not disappointed…

Follow John and his work here:

Rosalia

by
Demi Michelle Schwartz

Snowflakes dust me from head to toe as I follow the trail toward the cabin nestled in a grove near the foothills of the Rockies. Ice crystals crunch beneath my boots, the only sound besides the wind whistling between tree branches. My back aches from the weight of my pack and guitar, but I'm almost there. Soon, I'll settle into my home for the weekend and kick off my solo songwriting retreat with only nature for company.

Snap.

I freeze. Is someone following me?

My footprints are the only ones tracing up the slope, quickly becoming covered by fresh flakes spiraling to the frozen ground. A branch probably broke in the strong wind, that's all.

Leg muscles straining, I ascend the final yards to the grove, taking careful steps to avoid slipping on the ice. My nose and cheeks sting from the cold, my fingers numb despite being wrapped in fur gloves.

I halt on the summit to massage a cramp on my side. Snow coats the pine trees like powdered sugar, only a few vibrant green needles visible beneath. The setting sun spills into the clearing and illuminates the log cabin. Its wood emits a warm brown aura, the roof covered with at least a foot of snow.

I rock back on my heels, déjà vu flooding my body. The grove looks familiar, like a long-forgotten place I visited in a dream. I swear I've been here before. Weird.

Squinting against the sun's glare, I approach the cabin's door. It takes me a few tries to bend my stiff fingers and grip the knob.

An icy sensation swallows my hand, as though the wind's invisible fingers wrap around mine. Shivers lace my veins. The extreme cold must be messing with the nerves in my skin.

"Lia." The faint whisper of my name tickles my ear, as though someone is right beside me.

My heart pounds. I'm alone. My mind is definitely playing tricks on me.

I twist the knob and push open the door. The scents of pine, dust, and old wood waft up my nose. Golden sunlight filters through the foggy window above the brown suede couch. A beige-knitted blanket is draped over the back, and embroidered pillows rest on each side. Off to the right, a doorway leads into a smaller room, the bed draped with a thick quilt barely visible in the shadows.

A fuzzy memory floats from my subconscious. Moonlight pours through the window while I sit near the crackling fire, wrapped in a blanket and plucking the strings on my guitar. Only, the blanket is deep blue, not beige, and the guitar's wood is darker than mine.

Am I imagining things? I have to be. This is my first time here, and besides, the cabin couldn't be more perfect. I have my first studio session to start recording my sophomore album in three weeks, and writer's block has kept me from finishing a single song. Immersing myself in nature is exactly what I need. No distractions. No worries. Just music.

I close the door and cross the room. The wooden floorboards creak with each step. After setting my pack and guitar on the couch, I flick the light switch. The bulbs scattered across the ceiling stay dark. Is something wrong with the electricity? I turn on the heater, but no warmth seeps from the vents. I groan. This can't be happening right now. Why is my luck the absolute worst?

A shadow drifts in front of the frosted window. My spine stiffens, and I take an unsteady step backward. Fading sunlight silhouettes a tall figure standing stock-still. The person remains for a few long moments, then slowly moves from view.

I exhale a shaky breath. Who's out there? Probably just a hiker passing by, but a pit opens in my stomach. Maybe I should leave and go home.

No, I'm being ridiculous. This isn't the first time I've booked a solo trip in the mountains. I should be used to this by now. Isolation always comes with strange happenings. Once I get light and warmth, I'll write songs. Everything will be fine.

I face the fireplace, and my shoulders slump. There aren't any logs. Great, now I'll have to venture back into the cold to find some.

Sighing, I turn around. A slip of paper flutters out of nowhere and lands at my feet. Where did this come from? The ceiling? I crouch and pick up the page—a newspaper clipping. It's gray and faded. The text is hardly readable in the dim sunlight. This must be an article from a long time ago. Inspiration comes from the most unexpected places. Maybe whatever this is will spark an idea for the first song on my album. I step closer to the window for more light and read.

We're heartbroken to share the passing of Rosa Arianna Allegri from Knoxville, who was tragically murdered at age twenty-one while she was on a solo songwriting retreat at a cabin in Colorado's Rocky Mountains. A promising country artist on the rise, Rosa was a senior at Belmont University and had dreams of remaining in Nashville after graduation to pursue a career in music.

Rosa is survived by her parents, Giovanni and Alessia, and her younger sister, Isabella. A private funeral service will be held for family and close friends. In lieu of flowers, we ask for donations to the Rosa Ariana Songwriting Scholarship, which was established in her name. Gone too soon, Rosa's music will live on in all who knew her.

The obituary includes a black and white picture of a girl my age with dark hair, high cheekbones, and rosebud lips. She's standing in the famous circle on the Grand Ole Opry stage, guitar in hand, and wearing a light-colored gown with thin straps and a layered skirt decorated with polka dots, my favorite pattern.

My veins tingle. The girl looks familiar.

But that's impossible. I have never even heard her name before. The obituary is dated December 12, 1985, exactly forty years ago to the day.

My legs wobble, and I sink onto the couch. Why is this obituary here? I shiver. If I would change Rosa's family members' names and Knoxville to Boulder, this could have been written about me.

The cabin's walls fold in on me like they're trapping me in a casket. My palms itch in my gloves. Is this the place where Rosa got murdered? I read the obituary again, the paper crinkling in my unsteady grip. A cabin in the Rockies could refer to countless locations. There's no reason for me to assume this is the same one where Rosa died, and even if it is, this tragedy occurred decades ago.

The hair on the back of my neck prickles. I peer through the frosted window. A scream tangles in my throat, and I leap off the couch, sweat pouring down my neck.

A girl's reflection stares back at me in the glass.

Only, instead of my strawberry-blonde locks and green eyes, she has mahogany hair and irises such a dark brown, they're almost black. Her facial features reflect those of the fallen country songwriter on the newspaper clipping.

Rosa.

Gasping, I spin around.

But no one is behind me.

Throat swelling shut, I face the window again.

The reflection is gone.

I clutch my hands to my chest. Rosa's reflection wasn't there. I'm imagining things. The cold is messing with me. Rosa's obituary being here is a coincidence, nothing else. Maybe the last person who was here thought it would be funny to plant the newspaper clipping to scare the cabin's next visitor. Rosa just happened to be a songwriter, too.

I toss the obituary into the fireplace. Once I gather wood and ignite it, the paper will burn to ashes—out of sight, out of mind. The whole reason why I came here was to get peace and quiet before the buzz of the holidays to conquer my writer's block. I'm not going to let a piece of paper ruin this for me.

Still, the pit in my stomach won't disappear. I can't imagine getting murdered and having my life and dreams stolen away. Rosa may be a stranger, but I feel a deep connection to her now that I can't explain. I hope her killer was caught and her family got closure, but this is a reminder to live every day like it's the last. That's definitely a universal theme for lyrics. Maybe this weird situation will inspire a song after all.

I tap my foot at a slow tempo and hum a melody. No, too cheerful. This should have reflective undertones. Maybe I can make this song stripped back, just my voice and acoustic guitar.

But first, I need to build a fire before I freeze to death.

After adjusting my scarf, I cross to the door and pull it open. Brisk wind bites the exposed skin on my face. My hair whips around my shoulders. There must be fallen tree trunks in the grove I can use for a fire. If not, I'll have to settle for a pile of branches.

I trudge through the snow, studying the ground. Feet from the clustered pine trees, I pause, my lungs constricting.

Massive letters are carved into the snow. They must have been drawn recently, since falling flakes haven't buried them yet. I stumble back to get a better view of the full word: *Rosalia*.

I clap a gloved hand over my mouth. Bile rises into my throat. *Rosalia* is *Rosa* and *Lia* combined. Someone was here very recently and wrote this in the snow for me to find—someone who knows my name and Rosa's. Is this mystery person the same one who passed by the window earlier? Did they put the obituary in the cabin? That doesn't make sense. It appeared out of nowhere. I know for a fact I was by myself.

Heart racing, I stagger in a circle to take in my surroundings. The howling wind fills my ears. I'm alone with the trees, cabin, and snow.

But wait.

Faint footprints trace a path from the carved name to the base of a nearby pine. The impressions were made by boots much bigger than mine.

My chest squeezes. I have to get out of here. I can't blame the strange occurrences on my imagination any longer. Something is very, very wrong.

"Run, Lia," the same voice from earlier whispers into my ear, icy breath on my neck. "Run. Run. Run. He's coming."

My knees buckle. If I try to move, I'll collapse on the snow. Who's coming? I press my fingers into my temples. Hearing voices is never a good sign.

"Run. Now." The voice grows louder—a girl's voice.

Is this Rosa? I shake my head. No, I'm losing my mind.

Movement near the cabin catches my eye. I stumble over the carved word in the snow and grab a tree branch for support. Who's there? How do they know my name and Rosa's?

A tall figure steps into the clearing, cloaked head to toe in black. I yelp and grip the branch tighter. My heart thumps so hard, I'm afraid it will stop beating.

The newcomer inches closer like a monster stalking its prey. A bright flash hurts my eyes. I wince, blinking spots from my vision. Was that a camera?

No, not a camera.

The sunlight bounces off something shining in the figure's gloved hand.

A knife.

I scream and press my back into the tree. Tears trickle down my cheeks and freeze instantly in the polar temperature. No, this can't be real. I'm having a nightmare or hallucination.

The stranger charges toward me, knife raised. Whimpering, I race along the trees until I find a narrow path. My legs quiver as I bolt down the trail. Footsteps thunder behind me. I have to run faster, faster, faster.

Sharp branches and pine needles slice the skin on my face, but I don't slow down. Shadows crawl like unearthly creatures, the sun's last rays hardly peeking through the high treetops. The path weaves this way and that, and I keep my eyes wide open for obstacles.

A fallen trunk blocks the way. I clamber over it and hit the ground running again, my pulse thumping in my ears. I'm unsure how much longer I can keep this up. The woods are a labyrinth, and the stranger is a beast, hunting me down.

But I can't die.

I won't die.

My lungs burn. Each labored breath is a dagger to my chest. The path arcs, and I stagger around the bend. Sticks snap beneath my boots. The stranger's heavy footfalls pound closer, closer, closer. There's no way I'll be able to outrun them. I have to find a place to hide. They can't catch me. If they do, I'm dead.

The trail slopes upward. My thighs ache as I ascend. Keep going. I have to keep going.

A small opening yawns between two tree trunks. It will be just big enough for me to crawl into and tuck myself out of sight.

I jerk to a stop. My boot slips on ice. I shriek and windmill my arms. Gravity traps me in its inescapable force. I fall forward and slam into the ground. My frozen bones throb, as though they have shattered. No, I can't stay here. I have to move. Now.

I press my palms into the snow and drag myself toward the hiding place. A long shadow passes over me like a storm cloud.

My stomach drops.

They're here.

I sob and pull myself across the ice faster, my arm muscles straining. This can't be my end. I won't die like Rosa and have my music dreams stolen away from me.

The stranger jumps onto my back and pins me to the ground. My chin collides with the snow. A shard of ice pierces my skin, and I cry out. I thrash to break free, but I'm too weak.

My captor forces my head to the side, my cheek pressed into the ice. A ski mask covers their face, inches from mine. I want to scream at them to get off me, to let me go, but my voice won't work. Why are they doing this? Why me? I'm no one, just a girl with a dream.

"I thought I took care of you decades ago," the stranger says casually. His deep voice chills me more than the frigid wind ever could.

What is he talking about? I tremble under his weight. He must be mistaking me for someone else.

The knife glints in the dim light. In a swift motion, the man plunges the blade into my neck.

A sound I didn't think I was capable of making rips from my throat. My veins blaze, as though flowing with molten lava. Hot blood pours from the wound and soaks my scarf.

My vision darkens around the edges, my breaths slow and ragged. I grasp onto my thread of life, but it frays. My heart gives a painful thud. The woods become cloaked in inky black.

I'm standing in murky fog, the mist tinted blue from a distant light.

Am I dead?

I have to be. The final moments of my life flash before my eyes—the stranger, the chase, the knife, the agony.

I raise a hand to my neck. My fingers meet smooth skin where a gaping wound should be, and there's not a drop of pain in my body.

Where am I? Surely not the mountains. Is this the afterlife?

Tears sting my eyes, but they don't fall. If I had a beating heart, it would break.

My life, gone.

My dreams, no more.

All my friends and family will spend the rest of their days haunted by my murder.

The otherworldly fog shifts around me, gliding across my cheeks light as a feather, a soothing caress.

Who killed me?

And why did they think they ended me decades ago?

A silhouette approaches from the haze, their form haloed by the blue light. Their features come into focus—mahogany curls, dark eyes, pink cheeks, rosebud lips pulled into a frown.

“Hi, Lia,” Rosa says. Her voice floats like a forgotten melody, ancient yet enchanting.

I recall the strange occurrences before my killer chased me through the woods. “I heard your voice, didn’t I? I saw your reflection in the window. Did you give me your obituary and write in the snow, too?”

“Yes.” Rosa pauses feet from me, the mist swirling around us. “I was trying to warn you about what would happen. You see, I live within you, as you have come from me. I’m your past self.”

I gape at her. “My past self?”

She nods, and her curls bounce around her shoulders. “Together, we’re Rosalia. My murder was never solved. I got a premonition that my killer—our killer—would strike again. I wanted to save you from the same fate. I’m so sorry, Lia.”

I gaze into her eyes, and for a moment, I'm back in the log cabin, looking at her picture in the newspaper clipping. Was she familiar to me because she's my past self? I've never believed in reincarnation, but maybe the proof is standing right in front of me. Her brown eyes are windows into her soul—our soul. An invisible string tethers us together, a thread that can never be snipped in two.

And maybe this is why the grove looked familiar when I arrived. My soul knew I was there before. The brief memory I got playing a guitar by the fire must have been from my past life, when I was Rosa.

"What happens now?" I search for the source of the eerie glow, but it's coming from all directions.

"We have a choice," Rosa says. "We can either pass on, or return to Earth to solve our murders."

"You decided to come back last time, didn't you?"

"Yes." She traces her fingers through the mist. "But now, we can't be separated. We can either pass on together, or go back to solve our murders. You deserve to make that choice."

The blue light calls to me, shining like a heavenly sky. All I have to do is walk toward it in any direction, and we'll reach the afterlife, a land of eternal peace.

But Rosa and I have to unravel the mystery of our deaths. My case can't go cold the way hers did. Our families deserve closure, and our murderer needs to be caught and put behind bars.

I reach for Rosa's hand, half expecting my fingers to pass through hers since we're both ghosts. Instead, her skin is warm, as though life still flows through her veins.

"Let's go back," I say.

She smiles and squeezes my hand. "Are you sure you want to do this? Drifting around down there alone isn't fun."

“Positive. And you won’t be alone this time. We’ll have each other. Let’s solve our murders, then go to the afterlife together and write a song about it. The angels can be our backup singers.”

Rosa laughs, the musical sound out of place in this uncanny dimension. “Sounds like a plan, Lia. Let’s do this.”

The mist thickens. Hardly any blue light filters through the hazy veil. Hushed murmurs float from the shadows, like lonely spirits saying farewell. The floor vanishes, and Rosa and I plummet through the fog. We hold tight to each others’ hands as we spiral into darkness.

One day, we’ll return to this in-between realm and choose eternal peace. The blue light will reappear and welcome us to our forever home when we’re ready.

But first, we’ll find our killer and haunt him until he takes his final breath and goes to Hell.

Follow Demi and her work here:

The Shadow of North House

by Lee Swift

High Bradfield was heavy with snow when my husband and I moved into North House. The weather had been particularly bad that winter, and it made the decision to get into the place before Christmas a bit of an insane one, at least in my mum's eyes. She offered to take us in until the new year, but the level of enthusiasm I had for living in a box room at my own mother's house, with crates of our clothes, crockery, and lord knows what else, all stacked up around us for weeks on end; could have filled the tip of my little finger.

It was Jim and I's first real house together, and I wanted it to be perfect, all homely and snug, ready for when the baby arrived.

Despite the tough going - driving through banks of snow up the country lanes, the van sliding in the slush as we went; moving in winter wasn't *all* bad. The landscape was made all the more picturesque for the untouched blankets of white, patchwork fields that spanned the area.

Looking back now, I realise that moving in any other seasons would have allowed me to have a hint of the evil in North House, but in the event, those milk white snows became the Devil's alibi. They made the old oak in the courtyard seem as typically skeletal as it's brothers in the nearby woods. They covered the patch of soil, right below the bedroom window, that never grew a single blade, no matter how many times it was seeded. If you want to be unfair, you could say there was other signs too, like the fact that the Estate Agent was just a bit *too* eager, and the fact that the bedrooms were freshly decorated with geometric wallpaper and the latest laminate flooring, even though it clashed with the rustic feel of that old house. I'm an artist in my spare time, so those patterns of angled silver lines on the walls bothered the hell out of me when they were placed next to the sixteenth century house beams, but I was heavily pregnant, and other than the lack of taste in the bedrooms, I'd dreamed of a home like that since I was a little girl from Balby, so we took it.

When did things start to occur at North House? Well, that's a tougher question than you might think, because it relies on the fact that Jim and I recognised them as 'out of the ordinary'. If I had to hazard a guess, I'd say that place started working on us from the second we got to it.

I remember my mum commenting on how cold it was near the bedroom window when we were shifting the boxes in from the van. I was in the corridor, pacing up and down after the long drive. I remember feeling particularly antsy, as I wanted to help, but Jim insisted I didn't lift anything.

He was coming up the stairs as my mother was complaining and I watched him roll his eyes.

"Don't worry, Pat" he said, "the glaziers are already lined up for the work, first thing in January."

We left it at that, a simple dismissal of draught and age, but God help me, I think she was right. Every night, I would wake up, cold. I didn't dare mention it to Jim, because I was the one that pushed for getting into the place, and I could do without the argument, but, nevertheless, there it was, a subtle, almost imperceptible chill breeze on the air that penetrated the room.

There wasn't much beyond that in the run up to Christmas. I've read Shirley Jackson and I've a Netflix habit that's on the wrong side of healthy, so I know all the tropes of a haunting, but we were both exhausted from looking after Harper, our new baby, we just didn't pay attention. The evil that'd taken root at North House was subtle, so rather than going through every instance of a creak I heard on the stairs, I'll just tell you about the time, months later, when I first truly noticed it.

It was a warm day in April, and I was putting the ironing away. I was listening to my favourite podcast because lets be honest, raw-dogging ironing is about as boring as it gets, and the average conversations at the local mother and toddler group left me wanting something a bit more intellectual to say the least.

I'd decided to do it in our bedroom because of three reasons. First, I'd just put Harper down for a nap and wanted to keep an ear out for her, second, it'd keep me cool because I'd decided my mum was right and that room was cold, even with brand new double glazing fitted, and finally, it was a short trip from the ironing board to the wardrobe and I was feeling lazy. Sue me.

As I was going through the shirts, I looked at the wall which still held that modern geometric pattern wallpaper, when I saw something there. I took it as black damp, hid behind the dresser, barely noticeable against the slate-coloured paper.

I might have been tempted to do something about it there and then, especially seeing as we'd put off the stripping of the bedroom for a rainy day, but I heard Harper cry. It was like a sobbing, discontented cry.

I swear at this point, I know my own child's voice. She'd suffered colic from an early age, so I was always listening, always dreading that sound coming through the baby monitor, but that would always, *always* happen after we'd put her down for the night. This was a brief nap, long enough for me to do my housework.

I sighed and left the bedroom, and I swear on my life, as I opened that bedroom door, I saw a shadow moving through the door to Harper's room.

You never quite know how you're going to react when something like that happens to you. I can tell you I nearly shat myself, but I hesitated. I stopped in the doorway to my own bedroom, my fucking heart in my mouth. The background sniffles of Harper played on my ears and intensified as my entire senses prickled into full alert, searching for something, anything I could hear or see. The door to her room moved again, and I could see then, it was just that breeze, the one that played through the house, that seeped through the old farmhouse stones; it teased the door forward and back, it's movement casting the shadow I'd seen.

I cursed at myself for being stupid and started walking again, calling soothing tones to Harper before I'd even reached the door.

I was still a little shaken, so I was…I don't know…on edge as the door opened, ready for anything real or imagined. Thankfully, nothing was there, just Harper, her cot and the plush mobile of clouds and cows that teetered and played on the thinnest breeze. The odd part was that she was laid on her front, arms and legs sprawled, absolutely spark out.

I frowned. I listened, popping my head back around the corner of the door to try and catch her voice, but it was all silent, now.

I was scared, I can admit that, now, but when you're scared, it's amazing the lengths you'll go to, to convince yourself you're not. I berated myself for being such an idiot and even punished myself by refusing to watch a horror that night with Jim.

I returned to the ironing, cut the podcast off, and put on something a bit more wholesome, S Club 7, I think. I kept it at a manageable volume, my ears straining against the happy tune, listening intently for any more signs of the cries. None came, and I was secretly glad, when she woke up.

After cursing the Estate Agent, that weekend, I got Jim to strip the walls, treat them and re-paper, choosing something more fitting the look of a farmhouse. That made me feel a lot better, but the memory of what happened stayed in my mind.

I gingerly brought it up at the next toddler group with one of my new friends, Sherise. "Do you know if there's anything odd gone on at North House?" I asked.

Sherise was about four years younger than me, and if I had to sum her up in two words they'd be 'conspiracy theorist', but there wasn't anyone else I knew well enough to ask and let's be honest, she was the kind of person to know things like that.

"You seen something?" she asked, her face dropping serious.

"No, no, nothing like that. Well, no, I don't think so."

"Shut-up!" Sherise said, bursting to life with excitement as she played pat-a-cake with her baby boy. "You've seen something haven't you? What was it? A ghostly figure or like books flying across the room?"

"No, forget I said anything" I said, instantly regretting it.

"Oh come on" she pressed, "I promise I won't freak out."

Reluctantly, I told her, and of course, she lied. After her going on a ten minute safari of every ghostly apparition she'd heard or seen around South Yorkshire, I managed to get her focussed enough to tell me that North House was an old building.

"Wow. Like I didn't know" I said.

"No, you don't get me. I mean, it's *really* old. Older than any of the other buildings in High Bradfield. That's something people were saying when you bought it."

"People were talking about me?" I asked.

"Yeah, but not really in a bad way. At least I don't think so. They were just surprised because it's stood for ages, abandoned. I bet it was a right mess when you moved in, eh?"

“Actually, it wasn’t that bad” I said. “Estate Agents must have done some smartening up with it. Chose bloody awful decorating.”

“Estate Agents don’t work that way” Sherise said. “They don’t go around decorating houses. You get what you see.”

She had a good point.

“Well, yeah,” I said, “I knew that. I just thought they’d have worked on behalf of the owner.”

When I got back, I tried to find the owner through a deed search. It came up registered to the estate agents we used. I talked to Jim about it, but he dismissed it, said it was probably someone who worked for the company who had it and just used the company to flip it and make some money. I love Jim with all my heart, but sometimes, he’s so laid back it infuriates me.

I wasn't about to let it go. I called the estate agents and asked about it, but they told me they couldn't explain anything further. Gave me some crap about GDPR, data protection or something.

I wasn't happy, but with nowhere else to go with it, and with nobody else who cared enough to help me, I reluctantly let it go.

By June, the mould was back, again, this time obscured behind the dresser. Whereas before it was a faint, broken line, the unchecked festering had made it grow thicker, darker. The splinters of what I thought was mould joined together until they formed an unusual straight line, like it followed a path where the wood touched the wall.

Harper was six months old by then, and Jim was at a conference when I discovered it. I wasn't a helpless little housewife, though; he was more on the building and constructing arm of our duo, I was the designer thanks to my dabbling in art.

The second I spotted it, I was determined not to leave it to grow worse, so, as soon as Harper was down for her nap, I took my trusty scraper and got to work, determined to douse the bloody thing with the thickest bleach I had.

I hauled the dresser out of the way to find that the black damp only followed the rim of the dresser part of the way. There were more, disconnected patches spaced lower down, but still, it puzzled me as to why it didn't run parallel along the length of the dresser top.

Not being one of the big mysteries in life, I put it down to the fact that I'd either caught it in time as it was spreading for a single location, or that half of the wall had some way of keeping dry. Regardless, I went to the base of the skirting board and began stripping the paper away. Right from the start, I knew it was bad. The thing came off in great swathes, like butter that curled up over a warm knife.

"Shit" I groaned. More money to fix this.

The wall must have been so wet it barely gripped the paper. Sure enough, as it came away from the wall, black scabs of rot were clearly in the plaster, sporadic and varied. They eventually streaked upwards as I anticipated, rising the length of the dresser leg. But then, I noticed something odd. The line that first caught my attention was uncovered and it was thicker than the rest, more pervasive.

It was absolutely a straight line, and as had seeped through the paper, it stopped about halfway at the dresser. What I didn’t expect though is that the line that ran up from the floor parallel to the dressers leg intersected it and continued up beyond the dresser top, heading up the wall, disappearing underneath the most stubborn parts of the paper.

First curiosity grabbed me, then horror, as I stood back and looked at the shape that black mould had taken. It was a cross. An inverted crucifix. Anyone who was with me might have told me I was overreacting, seeing things. They might have said that my imagination had got the better of me from what happened a couple of months before. To that I’d say it was possible, but to me, the cross was far too uniform. Its points defined and even flared at the ends like the sign of the knights Hospitaller.

Whether the sceptics would have agreed with me or not, the sight of it spurred me on and their doubting mind would not have been able to explain what else I found, I'm certain.

I stripped more walls, the adjoining ones and the stubborn patches near the top and at the skirting. The sights horrified me and I gasped, but I carried on. To this day I don't know why, but I did.

There were signs everywhere.

I found words marked in the black spots of mould, written in Latin in discoloured patches. I found hand prints, too small to be adults, placed upside down, on the wall underneath the beams. I even found part of circle when I began panicking and tearing the carpet up from its tacs. It was at the window, that same one that emanated the cold breeze.

My brain was reeling and my instincts took over. I dropped everything I was holding and raced out of the bedroom, too terrified to even cry out.

I ran straight for Harper’s room, with the sudden visualisation that the gaudy modern paper had been put all the way around her nursery too. I was just about hysterical as I booted the bedroom door open, and almost collapsed with relief to see she was lying peacefully asleep in her cot.

The room had been redecorated at the same time as ours, but I didn’t waste any time confirming what I already knew. I grabbed her and bolted out the house without looking back.

I went down the hill to the Old Horns Inn, collecting myself as I held tightly onto my bemused, upset little girl. There wasn’t many people inside, it was a weekday, after all, but they must have known things weren’t okay. They didn’t pry, and I decided not to say anything. What could I say even if I’d have wanted to? They’d have thought me mad. I didn’t even call Sherise. I did what most people in that situation would do, I started convincing myself I’d overreacted, but I couldn’t deny the terror I’d felt and no matter what I said to myself, I vowed never to spend a second in North House alone.

The only person I called was my husband. I demanded he come straight to the Old Horns, and when Jim returned that night, we went back. My mum took Harper, but I gave her an excuse of a burst pipe, a fact she loved to point out was inevitable when we'd bought such a money pit against her advice.

Jim bless him was sceptical, but he could see how shaken I was. He didn't outright deride me, he reassured me, said he'd go back. I refused to leave him to it alone, so together, we drove back up the hill to that old house.

The place was dark and cold as you'd expect, but, I swear, as we opened the door, I heard a sound from upstairs like…like a babies cry. The sound of it makes my throat dry up and my palms go sweaty as I think about it. I didn't imagine it, because I know for a fact Jim heard it too. Any scepticism that might have been hiding in Jim's mind went flying out. He put on a brave face and told me to wait in the living room, but by the fact that he grabbed the claw hammer and torch from the back of the car told me he was scared, too.

I stood there, almost shivering, watching the ceiling as he called out and made his way upstairs.

It was nerve wracking to hear the crack of splintered wood and footfalls on the boards overhead, but doubly so, when the sounds stopped.

“Jim?” I called. Thankfully, he called back.

“Don’t come up here! Do you hear me?”

“Yeah, but why? You’re scaring me.”

“Just…just don’t come up here. Promise me!”

I hesitated, but I knew my husband’s tone was serious. He was scared.

“I promise. What’s going on?”

“N-nothing. Don’t come up here. Start packing the stuff up from the kitchen, whatever you can carry. We’re leaving.”

It was two hours later when he came back. In the space between, I heard footsteps on the floorboards, I heard the tearing of fabric and the gasp and grunt of effort. I think I even heard Jim cry at some point, but whenever I asked, he would just yell, scream down the stairs for me to stay put. When he emerged from the stairs, he had a handful of our things wrapped in a bedding sheet, along with our suitcase, and he grabbed me by the shoulder. I could see his eyes, manic and wide. I wanted to ask, demand that he explain everything, but I knew better. That night, without another word, we left North House.

Five years passed before he'd speak about what he found. He told me there were markings under the floor, like circles, pentagrams even, impossibly lined up precisely where our child's cot and our bed were positioned, yet he swears on our daughters life they weren't there when he had the carpets fitted. He said the hand marks and the inverted cross were still there, too.

I know he hasn't told me everything. He refuses to say what else he found, and insists there were no babies upstairs or recordings of any kind, to the point that he denies ever hearing a baby cry, but I catch him sometimes, looking at Harper in an odd way.

To this day, North House stands empty, and I hope to God it stays that way.

Follow Lee and his work here:

Withering Rose

by Phoebe A. Xavier

Quincy R. Abbot, the mastermind behind the bestselling Historical Fantasy novel '*Mehmed*',

had retreated to New England in the wake of that inaugural success. The book, about the first

Sultan of the Ottoman Empire battling vampires, was a phenomenal debut. Already the pressure was on for more.

He immediately sought a locale less stressful than the Volusia County fuckery he'd been contending with while writing *'Mehmed'*. As an English Litt professor at Stetson University he'd long ago settled into tepid tenure in the sprawling sabal littered along the St. John River, but it was turbulent. Bloody bar brawls and vicious alligator attacks erupted in them parts regularly, so he tried to play it safer than sorry.

Back then Professor Abbot interloped into the periphery of the NASCAR scene because he was so close as the crow flies. When it's right there why not cast a gander?

Moored inland in DeLand, the option proved a (sometimes pleasant) distractive jaunt.

Seriously scope expanding nights Quincy had had included: meeting white trash Wall Street brokers who'd gambled off thirty-three million dollars on the Daytona 500, hearing about four hundred pounds of weed washed up on the beach after the captain had fallen asleep at the wheel. He'd seen an innocent third gen Hells Angels kid get shot in the face behind the Noname despite the security budgets promised by reality TV, he'd smoked numerous bongs with nomad bohemians blissing out on the most frequented Bureau of Land

Management zoned tidal island used for rogue crab bakes.

Then later he'd narrowly dodged the ire of a gang composed of both illegal immigrants from the Caribbean and Embry-Riddle dropouts in a lost cashbag caper -- plus six other tropes ripped directly out of a Dorsey book that was reviewed by Hiaasen.

Abbot was rarely the hero in those anecdotes though, he mostly just watched it occur or had it handed to him second hand. Of all the gamblers he'd met, winners and losers, if any of them made either the right decision to stop betting *or* eight-hundred percent of the vig back on a longshot, they might not be the dullest sap to speed a hot fishing skiff down the Inner Coastal Waterway at four in the morning. And those were his friends in those days.

This menagerie of economics and discreet criminal culture was so complexly and perfectly Floridian that most of the world missed the joke. That zeitgeist stood unfucked in the themes he wrote about. It might've been a sad fulcrum but, *The Sunshine State* screaming for absolution was absolutely everything '*Mehmed*' was saying in its subtext. Straight facts he was just glad to be out of it, dismissed from that food chain as it were.

So he weathered his debut success twelve hundred miles north by north east of where he lived when he went viral, though, not far from where he'd grown up. Having been raised in Massachusetts, Abbot opted for the snug progressive haven of Brattleboro to regroup and start his next opus.

Brattleboro sat on the site of Fort Dummer, a 1724 British settlement on the land that would later be zoned as Vermont. Paddle upstream twenty or so decades later it was referenced in the HP Lovecraft story, *'The Whisperer In Darkness'*. Paddle up even further and you'd find it was a quaint little downtown draped over steep hills nestled beside a forking river. Farms, recreational sports and fine cuisine hovered about it within leagues.

At this point, three years after the initial Covid-19 outbreak, half the town had been bought up by New Yorkers fleeing a city of refrigerated trucks serving as morgues As the panic wore off and vaccines were synthesized, more than half the neighborhoods Abbot had found a rental in was converted to Airbnbs.

Despite heaps of snow in the winter, very few tourists were paying to be there during ski season. The lodges themselves had enough space to sell. Brattleboro was a bit more sunny day real estate; a classy looking place to pop into on your way elsewhere. Mud to Peeper season at least. In winter's grip it could be icy death.

After his first month as a Vermonter, Quincy was struggling to get a cohesive outline of the next book he was supposed to be writing down on paper. He hadn't negotiated an advance on the next project yet and only had about ten months at his current cost of living till he'd be broke again. If nothing else, Brattleboro was expensive.

In general it was draining the writer slowly - till he saw Rose. Then *she* began to drain him, conduits being evolved by then more specifically, paranormally, and permanently.

He first saw her on a late spring Gallery Walk night that happened to coincide with a new moon. On every first Friday, weather permitting, the whole town would coalesce for a celebration of art held in every art gallery and also in Harmony Lot.

Harmony was a cramped pay-for-parking lot at the nerve center of the town's business and cultural edifice. On a good night you'd meet a brilliant creative mind there honing or hawking their developing genius, on a bad night you could get stabbed by a junkie defending their right to give public blowjobs in front of your kids. Radical freewill, not the laws of voting folk withstanding.

Despite the inherent purpose of the pavement laid down in the 1950s, during Gallery Walk, public parking in Harmony was illegal. This allowed food and art vendors to fill the space instead. Being the biggest populace center within twenty-five miles, extending into Massachusetts and New Hampshire, it was a big draw. A place for DIY success, youthful mirth, and latter-day hippies treading water.

As a tipsy and presumably successful man perusing the scene, Abbot felt too comfortable devouring the physical forms of all the women younger than him which he saw as sexy. His deep blue eyes hid the glances he stole behind very expensive spectacles.

Most didn't discern the paltry lech for what he was as he lurched up Main Street from venue to venue. He still had about him well dressed airs of success and confidence as a shield. Ultimately though he wasn't charming or weird enough to mesh well with the bougie, granola cum laude people of Windham County.

A twenty minute uphill stagger returned him to the block his rental was on, Prospect Street. On the way he passed both youth in revelry and a handful of hobo vagrants who'd eyed him up for the value versus consequence of risking robbery. Quincy was a little too blitzed to recognize the difference in the danger just then, despite his Floridian tenure.

Then he rounded the house onto the driveway noticing her as she moved in the windows upstairs next door. The entrance to his partition of the house was situated on the left side of the first floor. He looked back over his left shoulder whilst inserting the key into the lock just then noticing her silhouette.

Rose in that instant was voluptuous and casually nude in low lighting. She pushed her hands through her amber hair suavely before spinning athletically off-screen, presumably towards her bed. A few seconds later the lights went off. Millennials and their voice commands to Siri, he thought as the key finally tumbled the lock.

The bestselling pervert let his stare linger on her windows a moment longer, wanting for a bit more debauchery till he gave up on ogling and went inside. Within, a narrow set of stairs wound tightly up to three-point-seven-five rooms – kitchen, three quarter bathroom, bedroom and a generous family room to view TV or entertain guests in. He stumbled up that steep climb home to his bed, forgetting her for a few hours.

When he awoke he thought he'd dreamed about Rose. She had been smiling, knelt on the bank of a stream until the water turned to thick whirlpools of maroon and someone or something screamed. A vision of unusual antlers, short swirling conical, resonated in his mind; a stomach was impaled by a sharpened bone. Chirping sounds kept him from getting back to sleep, alternately the annoying kids from next door on the other side or actual birds and squirrels battling for space about the large oak out back. He sighed as he creaked to waking life. At least he was in Vermont, not Florida.

Abbot did his best the next few weeks to ignore Rose but that was impossible. He ogled her each day, she was always in some window looking in some direction or other. It wasn't like she cared anyway.

She seemed sadly oblivious and distant, reading books with thick spines or typing whimsically on a vintage typewriter. A few times he would see the silhouettes of pictures left hanging in a dull red glow, clipped to strings in her makeshift darkroom after the shades were drawn back, but she never noticed him as he came and went.

Then he had another dream. They were in a mountain forest somewhere. Darkened woods, leaves rustling all around.

Rose was pulling her intestines out of her slit open stomach as he looked on in horror. She began to wrap the slimy excess of exposed intestines around his neck. Some force behind him that he couldn’t see yanked on the foul slippery noose of viscera till he was choking to death. Crying out for help only made him sink further into darkness until he thought himself dead.

Slippery oily blackness hollow unforgiving.

After that nightmare he made a concerted effort to not pry. He tried to avert his gaze every time he knew she was about, but her forlorn magnetism wouldn’t let him.

Some nights he’d look up and it looked like a series of abandoned rooms, no lights on, no signs of pictures drying out in the darkroom. On those nights he saw extensive cobwebs that might be gone in a day, then reappear fully developed again on another.

On one occasion the Ring cam pointing from the side of his rental across the driveway to her house captured Rose in surprisingly provocative undergarments getting dressed before dawn. It was uncanny. The cam activated not because of her, but because of a stray grey striped cat tiptoeing along the port side of her house. Precisely every thirty seconds the sly feline would move just enough to reactivate the Ring spotlight to ensure her half naked movements were fully lit.

Abbot went back to look at it the next day, confirming it was the cat that kept turning the flood light back on. It was a surveillance cultures' peepshow pervert vid of the week. Abbot plugged the footage into a video editing program he played with occasionally called DaVinci

Resolve. He edited it deftly and exported the session as a long .gif.

But he didn't dare to upload it anywhere. It was an attempt at a meme that nobody would accept, the unliked underbelly of Creepypasta and /NoSleep.

In September he took a bunch of psychedelic mushrooms and ambled down into the large, leased backyard to crumble onto a dilapidated wicker chair. He'd lit a fire in the safety of the fire ring the property owners provided. For a few hours he blissed out to music from his phone until an outburst from several dogs barking loudly disrupted his whole pseudo hipster groove. Looking in the direction he heard the barking coming from he noticed two small creatures near the back of the property. He recognized the tiger-striped grey cat curled up casually like a sphinx on break and next to him was an unusual raccoon. The raccoon stood upright and was chattering quietly pointing back and forth towards Quincy and Rose's homes.

To Quincy it seemed that the raccoon was showing the cat something they both had a vested interest in. They spoke in a real language, not in feral growls, meows or hisses. Nonetheless it was a language human ears could not comprehend. For hours he tried to figure it out but his mind kept playing tricks on him. He'd doze off for a minute then their chatter would wake him again, but they'd have moved into the oak tree or onto the deck.

For a few moments he slipped into a wet dream about Rose. He soaked her in: dazzling, beautiful. In black and white with her face cropped out of the frame, a million likes on Instagram. In real time with no filters or afterthought, a hundred thousand on OnlyFans. Which had better monetization? That would be the market standard.

Bloody fucking fucked either way.

That raccoon was eating his eyes out while he rubbed himself.

The fire had died when he startled awake in the chair disoriented. He tried to pretend that he wasn't spun cookies on boomers puking purple kittens. A deluge of Freudian analytical anxiety washed him in lust and he only got to sleep by chomping three Xanax and listening to a nine hour white noise video on YouTube.

He didn't dream for the next two weeks after that.

On Halloween the author was downtown for Art Walk again. He'd written almost nothing new, hence he walked up and down Main St. much less confident than he had been last time he was there. One of the galleries was showing a career retrospective for a local photographer named Bjorn Hellin. Quincy snuck in unnoticed and began to absorb the displays.

Bjorn was there at his exhibition, a stoic humble man who drew no attention to the fact he was the one that had taken all the pictures. He found it much more rewarding to watch the strangers' reactions to his art. Much of it would be evaluating micro expressions or half overhearing conversations.

Abbot R. Quincy stepped right in front of where the photographer was seated on an eighty-year-old stool. He stared at a photo pensively then gasped, "Oh shit that's her. That's the hot assed girl next door."

The two men both considered the photo that had elicited such a response. It was indeed Rose in a B&W photo, curly hair lounging on her forehead and about her face with a checkered scarf around her neck. She was pouting with plump pursed lips.

“You- you don’t know her. You’re not old enough to have known her,” Bjorn spoke up in disbelief, almost whining. It was the first thing he’d said in an hour.

“She’s my neighbor, next door upstairs.”

Bjorn hiccupped, asking through his nose, “Oh? No. What street?” Quincy answered perplexed, “Prospect Street.” Abject shock rippled through the old timer, his eyes edging wider as he said. “No... yeah, no. That’s Rose. Rose Arnoch. She’s… She’s n– she’s not around anymore.”

“I swear I’ve seen her many times over the last few months.”

“I hope you haven’t. Listen,” the photographer began, “I was friends with her in high school in the early 70s. She was a very talented girl, beautiful. A real hurricane with two dazzling eyes. But she held such sadness. One day her mother found her trying to hang herself when she was sixteen and they committed her to the Retreat for an extended stay.

She came back for a bit but she wasn’t all there. She went on a hike that summer and disappeared completely. Everyone knows she took her own life. But they never found her.”

Bjorn’s gaze drifted to the gallery’s bay window staring dully with a long frown. Awkward silence opened it’s maw between them and the writer left the older man to his sad thoughts. Another drunken uphill walk back to Prospect topped off the evening.

That night Quincy researched the Brattleboro Retreat. It was a psychiatric hospital and drug rehabilitation center that had been founded in 1834. He read about the Retreat Tower, a sixty-five foot cylindrical brick tower that had been built by patients in the late nineteenth century.

The doctors felt the view and the fresh air atop the monument would be therapeutic for the patients, instead it turned out to be a suicide leap point for numerous people. So the entrance was sealed up, but it remained an epicenter for suicides and paranormal activity.

He was beginning to see the real understated charm of the town. Some things he should have realized earlier started falling into place in his mind.

He noticed that he'd never seen her outside the house. Not once. He was only ever looking up into her windows. Nor was there ever any vehicle parked out front of the house or in its driveway.

The guy who came over to mow her front lawn lived across the street, but he never interacted with Rose. As far as Quincy saw then no one occupied the ground floor, though there was a magnificent backyard garden; despite it never being tended and intermittent storms somehow it was always resplendent with blooming vegetables, flowers, and foliage.

Another dream came to him, rife with gory visions of Rose slicing her arms open in a remote forest. He found himself on his knees before her as she began to levitate and pour her life force down into his eyes. Instead of being struck with fear he felt the dream a revelation.

In the morning he awoke with the first stirrings of an idea for a book.The next week he forced himself to complete an outline that he didn't completely hate.

The new book was to be called 'Sadsack Effulgence' and it was a road trip story that took from Kerouac considerably yet managed to have barely enough Quincy R. Abbot in it that he might afford to be an adult a bit longer. At best it was a sucker punch of hope that might work if given a chance. At worst it was a sign that he could still write. He forgot how early winter could set in.

Once it got colder he stopped seeing any signs of Rose. By Thanksgiving absolutely nothing stirred upstairs.

In early December the backyards were covered in snow and Quincy could see the finite extent of his savings looming up ahead like a thick brick wall. He also noticed Rose's house was now occupied on the first floor. She was an older woman who seemed to affect a surly disposition, yelling at the mailman and the neighboring dogs when they barked.

One day when he was coming up from the basement at the back of the house, climbing the short hill back towards his side entrance, he looked over and saw her staring at him. It was enough to make him lose his balance and fall over in a fit of bad adrenaline, some of the laundry got re-soiled.

She showed neither empathy nor satisfaction with his fall, just exuded displeasure. "We should get you a rope and you could pull yourself up," she snarled at him.

A wave of paranoia convinced his subconsciousness that her words were laced with undertones of suicide. She wanted him to hang himself he was sure of it.

A few days had passed when she came over with a tray of cookies as either a peace offering or an ulterior motive. She spoke kindly at first but he could see the disdain bubbling in her just below the surface.

He accepted the tray from her and dared to ask if she knew the girl who had been staying upstairs. Her face twitched and he saw the anger was back. “That poor girl had a horrible time in life,” she explained, “Her disgusting old grandfather beat and raped her when she was little and her parents did nothing to stop it. By the time she was twelve she was manic depressive.” “We call that bi-polar now” he mansplained, completely tone deaf. “Shut up, pansy,” she said, swinging her left hand to slap him in the face. The blow barely hurt but it shocked him. “You don’t get it yet. She knew that what he done to her was wrong. His old rotten brain made him do dysfunctional things. She didn’t want to ever grow old and evil like him. So she went hiking by herself out in the Green Mountains and slit her wrists. But a forestry serviceman found her and bound the wounds before she died. Plus she didn’t know about vertical/horizontal so that suicide didn’t take.”

"Hmpfh." Abbot raised his brows and cracked a fake smile like he knew he was talking to a crazy person. He was trying to correlate this version of the story against what Hellin had told him.

"Oh you think it's fucking funny do you?" she seethed, glaring at him with a throat slitting smile. The crone slowly tilted her head to one side holding the sinister grin.

Quincy recoiled a bit as he watched her jaw snap open to an unnaturally obtuse angle and her throat erupted, emitting a stream of brackish blood. He convulsed as the nasty fluid slopped his face, gobs of it in his mouth, eyes, and nostrils. The sense of dying again rushed into him and a foreboding blackness overtook him.

He awoke in his bed dripping in blood and bile. That wasn't a dream, was it? That really happened. Where was the realm of the real? What borderland reavers was he lost among? Reality was turning gooey, but he knew one thing. He had an adventure story he wanted to write buzzing around in his head.

The dizzy author showered and threw out his sheets, struck once again with a genuine inspiration to write. He was gonna write another book.

It was done in a week. He might have slept seven hours the whole time. Each instance he realized he'd lost the plot and succumbed to slumber he snorted another 120mg of Adderal. He was writing about himself but at the same time he wasn't. His taciturn year had reversed itself to an explosion of creative thought.

The novel poured through him. An exposition projectile vomited itself from him. He was but a vessel.

On the night he completed the manuscript he smoked a doobie on the side porch in celebration, the awning above protecting him from a light rain. The droplets hit in random syncopation creating a steady irregular rhythm. He looked into the backyard at the wicker chair by the fire ring. As his vision pulled in and out of focus he saw Rose sitting in the chair, her head was leaning at an unnatural angle as if her neck were snapped. He blinked twice and she disappeared.

All was right in the world.

A week later he heard back from the publishing house, his editor loved the manuscript. They wanted to ship it in New York Times Best Seller numbers. Abbot was chuffed. He'd done the damn thing. Twice now, he'd done it twice.

Splurge drinking champagne plunged him into one last dream about Rose. They were upstairs in her apartment which he'd been peering into for so long. She curled and cooed nude in her bed comforted by cush shag white fur sheets. Her vagina dripped sap as he looked on befuddled. Only by looking down did he realize he had a raging hard dick and a hand jerking it. Then he noticed something amiss. Wrapped in his fist as the buffer between his hand and phallus was a rolled length of sandpaper. He was shredding the skin off his dick, relentlessly horny for the ghost of this girl. A sinister siren that was fueled by contempt.

Sheer fucking razors to your eyeballs contempt.

He woke up after that nightmare to find he actually did it, he'd torn his dick to pieces. The sod had no idea where the sandpaper had come from, none should have been in the apartment let alone in his hand as he slept, but nonetheless his loins were a lacerated mess.

Quincy had such a disturbed sense of Zen that morning that he felt no actual pain. He calmly called the medics and shamelessly told them the wounds were self inflicted, even handing them the impossible sandpaper and the schmeg smeared on it. You know what they say? No pain no gain. Up is down, down is up.

After a few weeks of therapy and skin grafting surgery he was back to a new normal.

Painkillers got added into the mix of his other regular drug use and he felt fine.

He'd stopped wearing eyeglasses most of the day, unless he was reading something. He preferred that things be a little blurred so he could imagine they looked the way he wanted them to look.

The publishers PR firm had a slew of ideas on where and when to promote the book. In no time at all Quincy found himself on a popular late night TV show, hosted by the former head writer of Saturday Night Live. He hadn't been on television before and he was both nervous and pleased with himself.

A minute into the interview he stammered, looking down at his hands fidgeting in his lap. He looked up at the studio audience and was shocked to see every single seat was filled with a version of Rose, from her teen years to the older crone version of herself. Raising from their seats they wielded scissors, scythes, swords, dirks, axes and sundry other sharp pointy implements.

He looked back to the host but found that he had been replaced with a doppelganger of Abbot with his throat slit open. Dozens of Roses encircled him. The lights began to flicker as the first knife stabbed into his shoulder.

His life did not flash before his eyes as he was butchered, but several questions riddled his consciousness. Where was he truly? When had he left the Earthly Plane? Had he even written a second book? Was this an afterlife vision of Hell? Had he ever really been alive? Why was it ending?

If it were really the end. If there was ever any at all.

Follow Phoebe and her work here:

Road Kills and Chills

by

Anthony M. Caro

Come on, Clarence. Heads up. Literally.

If you stay passed out with your bleeding head on the steering wheel, you're going to burn to death. The scent filling your nostrils comes from gasoline fumes. Do yourself a favor that will last you the rest of your life. Again, literally - Heads up. Now.

The job isn't easy after hitting the windshield at 65 mph. Speeding in the rain in a sports car with a 355 hp engine isn't the best idea on well-maintained roads. Traveling recklessly on a winding dirt-turned-to-mud road because a torrential downpour boosted the hazards.

And those damn animals keep getting in front of the car. They make everything worse.

You can't blame them for trying to cross a muddy road at 3 AM. The cover of dark delivers the safest time for them to travel near the swamp.

You have something in common with those swamp denizens, Clarence. You sped your sports car down a dirt road to take the least traveled path to the far-off highway in horrendous weather under the cover of night.

Speeding in a flashy getaway car beats hanging around the place where you murdered three people. Then again, if there were a perfect scene for a murder, it would be a remote cabin in an equally remote swampy area.

You never know when someone will swing by a crime scene, so you anxiously hit the side road. A backpack filled with $50,000 in stolen drug money in the trunk of your sports car will understandably increase anxiousness, which can also increase distractions, contributing to unsafe driving.

Anxiousness and distractions are why you don't see that 3-foot-long baby alligator crossing the road until too late.

Wham. Splat. A 3-foot-long baby (Adolescent?) alligator departs this earth as your sports car's wheels - all four - run over the ex-reptile whose present physical condition can be described generically as roadkill.

Even with your distracted mind, you could see the remnants of other roadkill in your headlights. You did your part to add to the tally. The alligator wasn't the only animal you killed tonight. You nailed that damn duck that flew in front of you. The car's front hood clipped it, and feathers flew everywhere. Who knows? The duck might still be alive, but you aren't going to give it first aid. Likely, the poor duck ended up like the poor goose you caught out of the corner of your eye off the side of the road.

Lots of roadkill on that winding, dark road you sped down. Isn't it amazing that you could see anything when the unexpected torrential rain started pouring down faster and faster and furiouser?

Oh, Clarence, come on. You could've avoided that muskrat that you slammed into and crushed under your luxurious automobile. Admit it. You didn't care. All you want to do is get as far away from the crime scene as fast as possible. Besides, that muskrat is off to a better life Who the hell would want to forage for berries in this filthy and smelly place?

You smirked a little bit as you weaved around the road, almost flipping the car over when you hit a turn too fast. The right side of the car came off the ground about three feet, almost turning over, but the wheels returned to the road thanks to gravity.

You know, you have to keep your mind on the road. Maybe you can be forgiven because your mind's a bit occupied with having put three bullets in the three heads of three partners who helped to steal that drug money.

The time to get your head on straight was about 25 minutes ago. Anyone with a moral compass can't see the brilliance of shooting true blue partners and keeping the money for yourself. However, anybody with half a brain will ask you why you set fire to the hideaway cabin since it is in a remote section of a swamp.

First, they shouldn't judge you unless they have put three bullets into the heads of three people at 3 AM. Everybody wants to be a results player. They don't understand the euphoria and panic of having committed multiple murders when they've never pulled the trigger on people begging for their lives. Burn down the cabin seemed like a good idea because it could hide what happened until autopsy time.

It's a shame you didn't have your head on strong enough to realize that a fire burning in the middle of the night can be visible from miles away, so you ditched the scene pronto.

Next time, get a weather report before you commit multiple homicides. Pay better attention to the road, too.

Inclement weather and concerns over the fire department are the only things undermining your safe driving habits. That weird animal that crossed in front of your car snapped you back into reality - if you can call a state of confusion reality.

What the hell is that damn thing you only caught a glimpse of? It's hard to say with all the rain coming down, but was the rain coming down when that massive animal crossed in front of your car? The creature was large, grayish-white, and obscured by the rain.

At least, that's how you remember it in your foggy brain since you only caught it by glimpse. Your instinctive reaction was to swerve to avoid a collision with something too big too run over.

You avoided hitting the mystery animal, only to hit something else. That something else turned out to be a tree stump by the side of the road, causing your car to come to a brutal full stop seconds before your head hit the damn windshield.

Finally.

You wake up and lift your head off the steering wheel. Now you can smell the smoke from the car. You inadvertently "huff" gasoline fumes, which makes your banged-up head even foggier.

Better get yourself together, Clarence, because your car is on fire. That means the $50,000 and stolen drug money inside the backpack in the trunk is on fire, too.

Stop playing the damn accident victim. Hop out of the driver's seat, get to the car's trunk, and open it. Reach into your pocket and get the keys. You'll find out about your broken bones and other injuries once the adrenaline wears off.

You know you have at least second-degree burns on your hand as you with the keys in the trunk lock. You better get that trunk open and get that bag out quickly. The car is going to explode soon. You should've bought an electric one.

Great! You got the trunk open and the backpack out. The damn backpack is on fire, and that means the money is going to go up in flames soon unless you can put them out.

Time to get away from that damn car before it explodes! What's that smell? Is that swampy water? Yes.

The flames from the vehicle illuminate swamp water off to the left. Time to run to that smelly water and submerge the burning bag before worrying about how to get out of this situation. Calling for roadside assistance is not an option.

Perform the immediate task - submerge the flaming bag in the shallow water at the road's edge.

Good job, Clarence. The fire is out. But you should've held onto the backpack straps a little firmer. Some animal hooked around one of the straps. It's moving away, taking the bag into the swamp water.

Clarence, you have the most awful luck.

The damn backpack gets away from you faster than you thought.

You don't think a dumb animal knew what was in the bag and decided to run off with your money, do you?

Call it more bad luck going your way. And your bag is going away along with all your money if you don't chase it. Not that it's a great idea to jump into swampy marshland, but what choice do you have?

Not all the embers on the bag burned out. Part of the bag didn't entirely submerge, and you can see orange/red embers illuminating it slightly in the darkness. You had better hurry and chase after that thing because it will disappear soon.

What the hell is dragging it? Hopefully, it's like one of the ducks you hit with your car,

not one of the small alligators. Running into more ducks wouldn't be that bad. Running into a bigger alligator that has the potential to be extremely bad.

What do you want to do, Clarence? Do you want to cut a lousy night short and start running on foot? You have to do that with or without the backpack and your money. The combination of a rattled brain, blood loss, gasoline-fume high, and greed get you chasing the bounty.

Where are you going? Looks like you made up your mind. You're not letting that bag be dragged off into the watery swamp, leaving you with nothing to show for all your hassles.

The water is not very deep. We are only talking 10 to 14 inches, although you sink slightly in the mud. You trip and discover there's more than mud in the water when your knee hits a sharp stone.

That happens when you trip on a jutting tree root in the marshy swamp. You aren't hopping around in a wading pool—Rocks, roots, and who knows what else hides in the swamp.

Get off your knees and chase that damn backpack before you lose it! You lost it. Now, there it is again. It dipped behind a tree, and you better run to the bag before the money's lost.

The burning fires from the car illuminate the area and lend a hand to the moonlight, doing very little to assist you.

Boom!

Look behind you!

Your sports car finally blew up in a ball of flames. At least it's giving you enough light to see a bit more in the swampy marsh.

You turn your head to look forward to see how much additional light you're getting. The light is helpful, but you are far from the burning car. Not helping matters is you lost track of the backpack when you turned your head.

The lighter. The lighter. Check for the cigarette lighter in your front shirt pocket. Mercy. It didn't fall out. Flick it. Pray that it's not wet.

It's not!

The small flame helps you see in the shadowy areas shrouded in darkness. All you can see are trees, vegetation, moss, lily, pads, muddy water, and many shadows.

Are those shadows?

What else would they be? Your lighter's flame will cast shadows, much like the flames from the car. What interesting shadows they make. One of them looks like the shadow of a muskrat, which scares you. You turn around and swing the flickering light but see nothing in the water.

How odd that the shadow is up in a tree and not at ground level. You lower the flame to see what is near your sinking in one foot of water shows.

The lighter flame reveals…roadkill floating in the water. Even in the limited light, you can see rats, water moccasins, ducks, geese, raccoons, possums, and the ever-present baby alligator.

All display the telltale signs of a tire running over them. They are definitely roadkill, but what are they doing so far in the swamp?

You look up again and notice your flame is casting shadows on tree branches – shadows of the road kill.

Forget about that. Look for the backpack and the money. Make an arc with the lighter flame.

The near heart attack you feel makes you wish you didn't. Your heartbeat subsides to normal when you realize the corpse of a human being, a man ripped to shreds from claws and bite marks, isn't there anymore. He was there a split second ago. No, he wasn't. Your mind played tricks on you.

Did you hit your head bad enough that you're hallucinating?

Your occupied mind isn't thinking about the backpack and the money right now. The roadkill collective is also gone. Looking up, you notice their shadows remain.

Aren't shadows solid black? Things are different in the swamp, but they won't be so different that shadows become gray and white. Shadows are also solid, not see-through. They have to be shadows. What else could they be? Ghosts?

Your mind's flying south. The flickering flame on your lighter is starting to die because the fluid is running low.

Look around for that bag, and if you don't see it in the next two or three minutes, it's time to start the long walk out of here. The backpack you don't see, but hallucinations of oversized roadkill become hard to miss.

A 6-foot-long, dead alligator isn't oversized. Call it average. Your heart doesn't skip a beat because you've learned to stop caring about figments of the imagination.

Frustration sets in. It's time to put an end to all these hallucinations with a proactive step.

You kick the shadowy roadkill alligator, expecting your foot to go right through it, hopefully discouraging future hallucinations.

The only thing you succeed in doing is hurting your foot when you kick a solid living alligator.

Wham!

The alligator's tail hit you in the leg, knocking both feet out from under you. You know enough to extend your arm to keep the diminishing lighter flame above water and from going out.

Looking up, you see the ghostly roadkill shadows in the trees once again. You finally find your backpack. It's hanging from a branch in the tree, surrounded by roadkill shadows.

If you were the superstitious type, Clarence, you think the "shadows" had led you to this spot. You're not the smart type, either. You made the mistake of traipsing around in the swamp by yourself.

As the lighter's flickering flame goes out, you remember you're not alone. An alligator smart enough to avoid crossing the road at night reminds you that you have company when it takes a big bite out of your leg.

One bite. To start.

Follow Anthony and his work here:

The locket

by
Colin C. Martin

The sound of marble chipping and breaking echoed around the crypt. The restful silence of the dead was broken by the frantic pounding of a sledgehammer. Eric was breathing hard, physical labour was not his forte. The rivulets of sweat and flushed features showed a man who was more used to operating a keyboard instead of a builder's tool. Yet here he was having broken into a mausoleum and now trying to crack open that bitch Levin's tomb.

Eric didn't want to think about the prison time he might be facing. Was grave robbing still a crime committed these days? He wondered briefly, almost laughing at the absurdity of this random thought now intruding into his head. Sure, what was a little jail time? Especially if it finally meant an end to the torment he was being subjected to. Anyway, he wasn't here to steal or to take. He was here to return something that belonged here. Something that he shouldn't have been mixed up in, yet here he was. Eric paused to catch his breath and found himself reflecting on the circumstances that had placed him in this insane scenario.

It was a bright, September day when Eric found himself walking down the main street of a Wiltshire village. He was heading home from an area meeting which his firm held every quarter. Eric liked to take a break when he could from the main towns and cities. Working in sales he spent his days constantly in the hustle and bustle, always having to maintain a high energy as he looked after clients, trying to get that extra contract or add-on package. It was nice to take a step back from it all, even if it was for only an hour's stop before driving back to London. Once he returned, the grind would start up all over again.

Despite Salisbury and the surrounding area being major tourist destinations, attracting thousands of visitors, who passed through each year. The county managed to maintain an old world, out of time feel to it. Eric surmised that this was due to the location and history of the area. It was a quirk of the region as opposed to any kind of design. He knew too well that any corporate attempt to create this type of 'authenticity' would always fail, generating instead something feeling cheap and manufactured.

There was a feeling of magic to the area as well. Anyone that ever passed through the region couldn't deny experiencing it. Maybe it was the proximity to Stonehenge and the cultural remembrance of ancient pagan practices and folklore. Noone knew for sure. It was some of that magic that Eric was looking for now. Linda, his wife had her birthday coming up. She was a potter who had a small boutique store where she sold her wares and other trinkets. Eric still found himself amazed at how, even after ten years of marriage, they still managed to balance and centre each other. Considering their completely different backgrounds and vocations, this union should not have worked, but it did. It was at these times that Eric liked to try and put some thought into a unique gift for her. This time, however, would prove to be a mistake.

The bell sang as he opened the door of the antique store and entered. Eric paused briefly to look up at the device before fully stepping into the premises. The mechanism itself was straightforward. It was the bell that caught his attention. By the looks of things, it was made of solid brass. He could have sworn that he felt the weight of the bell as he passed under the door. Intricate symbols were embossed on the outside and inside of the bell. Erick could make out the shapes of runes scattered in a seemingly random pattern over the surface. He couldn't even begin to guess what these meant. They looked good and felt right, somehow. Eric shrugged and continued to walk into the store.

"Ahh! I see the clocca has caught your eye". The voice came from an elderly gentleman standing behind the shop's counter. While not an overly tall man, he stood straight and projected an air of authority and command. His white, wispy hair spoke of a lifetime of adventure and discovery. At least something more than simply succumbing to the aging process. He wore a crimson waistcoat over a neatly pressed black shirt. It was striking, but not overly theatrical. He looked around his surroundings with something akin to a general surveying his troops as opposed to a simple proprietor checking his wares. Eric found himself suitably impressed by the gentleman and walked over to chat with him.

"Yes, it seems a little on the extravagant side for a door's bell." Eric said. The shopkeeper seemed amused by his response. "Indeed, it would be if it was just there to alert me to visitors." He said. "A clocca, this one was made to ward off evil. The ringing cleanses the air when you enter.

The intention is to remove ill will and feeling from our visitors, allowing you to have a moment of peace while you peruse our items. In this madcap world don't we all need a moment of peace?"

Eric was in complete agreement with the sentiment. One of the reasons that he visited these places, apart from picking up something for Linda was to have a moment of solace. He appreciated the gesture, even though the cynical side of him saw it as part of the sales pitch. "It is indeed." Eric answered. "It's a nice touch and quite memorable. I don't think that I've visited here before. This isn't normally my stop on the way home. I'm glad that I discovered you." The shopkeeper smiled. "You are more than welcome! We are a little out of the way off the beaten, tourist track. I prefer it this way, especially as I advance in years. Dealing with hordes of people can be a little taxing." Eric nodded. "Oh I agree, that's why I buy most of what I need online, large stores can be a little chaotic. Not my cup of tea at all." The shopkeeper smiled again in agreement. "Well, seeing that I have a few moments of your precious time, how can I be of service?"

Eric explained the reason for his visit. He talked about Linda and the fact that her birthday was coming up in the next couple of weeks. He described a couple of the items he had picked up in previous years and her reaction to them. The shopkeeper nodded and smiled as he described each item. Eric had a strange feeling that something else was going on as he talked to this gentleman. He had never gone into such detail before when enquiring about a potential gift for Linda. Somehow though, this manner of parlance seemed to be expected, as if it was necessary to be able to proceed. When he had finished his recounting the shopkeeper nodded in understanding, as if something had passed between them. “Yes, I can see that this is a special woman in your life. I may just have what you are looking for.”

For a man advancing in years, the shopkeeper seemed quite spry as he moved from behind the counter, leading Eric to a glass cabinet at the back corner of the store. His voice carried the hint of gleefulness as he began to talk about the items.

"You will see here various pieces of jewelry that has come into my possession over the years. Not your average 'antiques' that have been picked up at car boot sales or auctions. No, each piece has a story attached to it. Sadly, not all the tales are happy ones, for example this necklace."

He unlocked the cabinet with a small key that he kept on a chain attached to his waistcoat. "Let's see." He mused. "I think this might just be the piece for your good lady." He lifted out a small box displaying a silver necklace and pendant. Interspersed along the links of the chain were small diamonds with slightly larger versions of the stone adorning the pendant itself. Eric was impressed.

Just as he picked up the piece to have a closer look a glint of something caught his eye. Glancing across towards the cabinet he saw a broach sitting towards the back of the display cabinet, now revealed when the shopkeeper removed the necklace he was holding. It had bronze, golden texture to it and was studded with what looked like miniature pearls. At the centre was a round onyx stone setting off a contrast against the rest of the piece. Eric found himself intrigued. "What's that?" He asked. The shopkeeper looked to the spot where Eric had indicated before frowning slightly.

"Oh, that. It's a simple locket. To be honest with you, for the price I wouldn't deem it as anything of great value. I purchased it from friends of the family who had to sell it under less than pleasant circumstances. I'd meant to keep it myself, but something's compelled me to place it on display. Now the piece you are holding……"

Eric didn't hear the rest of what was said. He had his eye on the locket now, there was something alluring about it. Maybe it was the simplicity of the design. He knew that Linda wasn't fussed on what she called 'flashy' jewellery, which the piece he held bordered on being. He guessed it wouldn't hurt to compare the pieces. "I'll just have a quick look, if you don't mind." He said.

Before he knew it, Eric was in his car driving home. The last 20 minutes of his life seemed to have gone by in a blurry fog. He was aware that words were exchanged between himself and the proprietor of the store. He knew that he was reluctant to sell and the price was well above what he would usually pay for a piece like this. The locket didn't even have a chain and yet he knew that he had to have it. After some back and forth, he bought the locket and a small chain the seemed to match its aesthetic.

He would source a decent presentation box when he got back home, there was still a bit of time before Linda's birthday. Traffic was reasonable on the M4 and Eric made good time, making it back just before the sun started to descend. Linda was home, having finished up for the day. A casserole and bottle of their favourite red was on the table.

"Thanks honey! You didn't have to wait for me, you know these dopey meetings eat the day away. How's you?" Linda was an attractive, slim built woman in her late 30's. Her shoulder length, blonde hair seemed to always sit perfectly on her square shoulders. She had a litheness about and a toned arms gained from working with her hands every day. She wasn't one for wearing a lot of makeup or wearing flamboyant clothing, a look a lot of her 'artist' friends seemed to embrace. Eric smiled when he thought of how gaudy they looked compared to his wife's simple elegance. Even without trying she always had a certain style about her. 'Some people just have it.' Eric thought.

The evening went quietly and comfortably as usually was the case when Eric got back. They exchanged quips about their working days while settling in for a spot of television before bed. Eric had slipped the broach and necklace into his sock drawer. He was sure that Linda knew where he stashed her presents, much like he was aware of the bottom, right hand corner of her wardrobe would hold certain gifts throughout the year. Both respected each other's privacy and forewent the temptation to peek. It was part of the marriage ritual after all.

One which had held them in good sway throughout their years together. Which is why Eric found himself more shocked than annoyed when he found his wife holding the broach in their bedroom a few days later.

"I'm sorry honey, I couldn't resist peeking." She said. Although he couldn't quite put his finger on what it was, Eric could see that there was a change in demeanour with his wife. She had an almost hungry look in her eyes as she traced her finger over the surface of the locket. It was if her fingers were tasting the indents made by the embedded stones. 'At least she likes it.' Eric thought.

“Ahh, well honey, it looks like the jig is up. I suppose I don’t need this anymore.” He produced a simple, yet elegant jewellery box from the inside pocket of his jacket. Linda smiled at him. “Oh, my dear! I’m feeling a little embarrassed now. I don’t know what came over me. I know you put a lot of effort into finding interesting things for me. I’ve spoiled things now.” Her face dropped and Eric couldn’t help himself but put his arms around her. No matter the circumstances, the last thing he wanted was to see Linda upset. “Don’t worry, at least you saved me from having to wrap it, you know I’m useless at that. I suppose now that you have it, you might want to put these inside the locket.” He produced two, passport sized photographs.

“I managed to get these printed at the chemist. They have a photo lab and were able to reduce these to make it easier to cut into shape and fit inside. I was planning to get this all done over the weekend.”

Linda smiled as she looked at the prints. "That time we went to Malaga." She mused. "Good choice, let's get them placed." They went down to the kitchen to make use of the table, Eric grabbing a pair of scissors from the drawer. The catch on the side of the locket took a bit of work, but eventually they pried it open. Inside were two black and white photos of a man and a woman. The period dress hinted at something from the 19th century. "That's funny." Linda said. "He looks a bit like you." The resemblance was uncanny, Eric thought. Life certainly was full of strange coincidences. They carefully prised out the photographs and looked over them. On the back of the man's was the initial 'J'. On the lady's was the initial 'E'. Eric perked up. "Jonathan and Edna! I remember the proprietor mentioning their names when showing the item to me. He said something about them having a tragic back story, hence he was reluctant to sell. Well, here's to a happier future with this little thing, eh?" Eric quipped. "What will we do with these?" Linda asked pointing to the old photos.

"It seems a waste to throw them away, they are a piece of history." Eric nodded. "I could post them back to the antiques store. The owner seemed to have a connection to the family. He could pass them back or keep them himself. I'm sure that he would appreciate the gesture." Linda gave her husband a peck on the cheek before saying. "That's a good idea love. I'm sure he will appreciate the gesture."

Life went on as usual over the next few weeks. Linda celebrated her birthday with Eric and some of their close friends and family. Work for them both fell into the usual rhythm and things seemed to be going well. That was until the nightmares began. Eric and Linda weren't huge drinkers. A few glasses of wine at the weekend and they were happy. They had followed pretty much the same routine on that Saturday evening before heading to bed. To drink enough to cause blackouts or hallucinations was not even remotely in their wheelhouse. Eric couldn't remember what roused him, whether it was a cold rush of air or a sudden noise. The last thing he expected was to see an apparition looming over Linda's side of the bed.

At first, he didn't know what to make of it. Thinking maybe it was a trick of light and shadows he squinted over at the supposed looming shape. Tired curiosity quickly turned to shock as he made out the shape of a woman in a black dress leaning over his wife. Eric quickly sat up trying to register what he was looking at. "Wha, ahh, um!" Was all he was able to blurt out before the shape disappeared. His movements and muttering stirred his wife. "Are you okay love?" Linda asked. "Yeah, yeah honey. I think my imagination is just playing with me. I got randomly startled is all."

Eric tried to chase the incident from his mind as he carried on with his working life. One thing that he couldn't ignore was Linda's behaviour. As the days went on, she became more distant. It was as if something was on her mind or occupying her attention. He would come home to find her sitting at the kitchen table staring off into space. 'Maybe she has an important piece of work that's been commissioned.' He thought. He tried asking her a few times but was only given the frustrating answer of "It's all fine honey!". Hoping that she would come around or tell him what was happening, he decided not to push the issue.

It was during his tea break at work, when Patricia, one of their close friends and a colleague of Linda's called him. "Sorry to bother you Eric, I'm just checking in on Linda. She hasn't been at the studio for the last couple of days. She didn't mention being sick. I hope everything's okay?" Eric was a little taken aback. "Um, she seemed fine this morning, although I did leave early. Maybe she picked up something and didn't want to bother me. I'll check in on her. Thanks Pat! I appreciate you checking up on her. You've always been a great friend!". Hanging up the phone, Eric realised that he had to get to the bottom of this. It was easy enough to book the day off, he wasn't usually absent. Tim, his supervisor, was understanding when Eric told him that Linda had suddenly taken ill, and he had to bring her home. Taking a few moments to tidy up his workload, he then jumped in the car and headed home.

Linda was once again sitting at the kitchen table. Instead of staring off into space this time, she was holding on to her locket, caressing it with her index finger. The look on her face was of intense concentration and she never even registered Eric's arrival or attempts to talk to her.

“Honey! What’s wrong? Everyone’s worried about you. Patricia called. She says you haven’t been to work. What’s going on? I know something is up, this has been going on for a while now.....” The words came tumbling out of Eric’s mouth as if their release was letting out the pent-up frustrations of the previous month and a half. He couldn’t understand it everything had been fine, they never had any issues like this until after her....

Birthday!

The sound of the penny dropping almost sent a clanging in his head. ‘No! That’s crazy!’ Yet, there she was staring at and caressing the locket as if it was Tolkien’s fabled ring of power. He looked at Linda’s eyes now, they were just staring but glazed over. Strangely enough they looked as if a white, milky film had started to form over them. Not being a massive horror movie fan, he had seen enough trailers pop up to recognise how they depicted people who were possessed. “Linda. Can you set that thing down for a moment please? We need to talk.” As he spoke to his wife Eric gently clasped his hand around the locket.

Whack! A force like nothing he had ever encountered before sent him barreling back. He landed with a thump on the kitchen floor, with the wind knocking out of him. Even while in shock after what had happened Eric could still appreciate the unnatural speed with which his wife jumped from the chair to land on top of him. "YOU AREN'T GOING TO LEAVE ME AGAIN JONATHAN. IF I CAN'T HAVE YOU THEN NO ONE CAN!" The words that came out of Linda's mouth weren't hers. Despite the terror, Eric knew this instinctively. This wasn't even the sound of a woman shouting. No, this was an echo from somewhere else. In that moment, Eric felt the call of the afterlife, hell or quite simply death. That voice was not human, and it came from a place not meant for mortals. His bladder gave out and Eric felt the warmth spread through his trousers. He was no hero, but neither was he a timid man. What shook him now went deep into his very being. He could almost taste the rage and hatred. Was this what pure evil felt like?

He managed to shake out of his reverie, just as Linda's hands started to clasp around his throat. Her fingers felt like ice as Eric felt them press in and start to cut off his air supply. 'Not like this.' He thought. Linda was a kind-hearted person, there was no way on earth that she was capable of this.

His mind was racing, going over recent events looking for clues to what caused her breakdown. 'Her birthday, the locket. She called me Jonathan. Wait? What was the woman's name? The one in the other picture. Don't black out now, think. Think!'

"Edna" he managed to croak out. His voice raspy and carrying the desperation of a man facing his demise. Air rushed into his lungs as he felt the pressure released on his windpipe. A strange expression appeared on his wife's face. It wasn't love or affection. It was almost that of a predator showing curiosity at its prey. Like a cat playing with a mouse that it had just caught. "Jonathan? You've come back to me?" The disembodied voice queried. Eric's fist lashed out before he even knew what he was doing. Despite being in the odd tussle during his school days he had never actually been in a proper fight before. The speed and ferocity that he threw the punch shocked him almost as much as it did the Linda/Edna hybrid thing in front of him. Her eyes momentarily showed confusion before they closed, and she slumped to the floor.

Adrenaline was coursing through Eric's veins now. He was almost at the point of hyperventilating as he scrambled out from under Linda's unconscious body. She wasn't a heavy woman, but her dead weight now felt like it was crushing him. Was this something strange and supernatural as well? Eric couldn't believe how calmly and rationally he was accepting the fact of a ghost was possessing his body, or how openly he felt right now about the spirit realm in general. Maybe it was Linda's wicca friends that he would at special events when he helped at her store, or their friendship circle at large that had gently prodded him into the realm of belief. Maybe it was the disembodied, demonic voice that had just reached into his soul while his wife casually tried to kill him that convinced him.

He knew that he couldn't waste any time. His wife may never forgive him when she came to and this could be the end of their marriage, but Eric would rather endure that than let her get taken over by this thing that meant to do her harm. He quickly lifted her up and carried her into the living room, placing her gently on the sofa. Her grip on the locket had loosened, so he took the opportunity to snatch it from her hand. Strangely he felt a pull as if something was holding it to her palm. 'Linda's consciousness must be giving this thing strength.' He thought.

Grabbing his car keys and jacket he knew where he had to go.

“What the hell did you sell me?” Eric shouted into the speakerphone as he hurtled down the motorway. He had to be careful, no matter how desperate he was not to exceed the speed limit. The last thing that he needed to happen right now was to be pulled over. “Sir! I’m afraid I don’t know what you are talking about.” The voice of the antiques store’s proprietor squeaked from the other end. “You know fine well. This isn’t a time for playing games. My wife’s life is in danger. The Locket, you didn’t want to sell it to me. I didn’t listen. I’m sorry you must tell me. Please! How do I fix this? I’m heading to you now. I have it with me.” The line went silent for a moment. Eric had to wipe the tears from his eyes that had begun to pour out. He realised that this man was his only hope and if he cut him off now and left the shop, he would have nothing. The sense of dread was starting to overwhelm him.

“She wasn’t a kind person.” The shopkeeper gave a sigh of resignation as he prepared to divulge the details. “Edna was a second cousin as far as I remember. The details of the murder were held back from the tabloids at the time, thanks to her title and family connections. Instead of causing a fuss, the Ladbroke family were paid off and Edna quietly admitted to an asylum to live out her days. It was said at the tribunal that she broke down and lost her mind. When the family visited her home, they found strange writings and tomes on black magic and witchcraft. The last thing that they wanted was the scandal if any of this got out, so they kept it quiet. It was bad enough the rumours and gossip that went around the local village about the ‘Black Witch in the Castle’. The Levin name had to be protected.”

“I don’t care about any of that.” Eric was surprised at how sympathetic he sounded. Maybe his skills as a salesman were kicking in. Subconsciously, he realised that this was a pitch that he had to close. Linda’s life and maybe even her soul depended on it. “I just want to help my wife. Linda is in danger. I can’t describe what I saw. You wouldn’t believe me in a million years. I just know that if I don’t fix this now, she’s gone forever. Please tell me what to do.”

The shopkeeper sighed again. Eric would later muse later that maybe he should conduct more of his tele sales calls while on the brink of madness whilst hurtling down the M4 at 70 miles per hour. His figures would be off the chart. “Do you have the locket with you?” He asked. “Yes” Eric replied. “I took it off Linda after I had to knock her out cold. She tried to kill me.” Eric could almost sense the shopkeeper nodding at the other end of the line. “If she’s unconscious then there may be some time. Don’t bring the locket here. You need to give it back to its owner. Here are the details.”

Eric plotted the location of the cemetery into his Sat Nav. After a quick stop to B&Q to pick up a sledgehammer he arrived at the crypt a few hours after closing. The questioning look of the cashier when he purchased the tool reminded him that he had soiled himself earlier. He wondered if at this stage he looked like somebody demented or had he just passed enough for an average person for her not to have called security. Maybe she just didn’t care and didn’t feel like she was paid enough to deal with the drama. In any case he’d managed to here and was more than ready to end this madness.

The marble cover of the crypt niche finally cracked and fell to the floor in heavy pieces. The coffin lodged inside looked well preserved. Eric briefly mused that the stone structure helped to preserve everything and stay the rot. He steeled himself and wrenched the coffin free from its holding place. The wood splintered and broke as it crashed onto the floor. Eric unceremoniously kicked at the lid, knocking it off. He almost gagged at the sight of the body. Apart from the odd family funeral corpses weren't something that Eric came across on a regular basis, especially not in this state of decay. Once he got over the shock of the sunken, leathery skin and the gaping mouth he could quite easily make out the form of Dame Edna Levin. The remaining shredded pieces of black cloth instantly brought the image of woman from the locket's original picture to mind. Eric wondered for a second what could have led this woman down the path that she ended up traveling and if at the time she thought that it was worth it. He bent down to place the locket around her neck.

Eric was knocked backwards by the scream that rang around the chamber. The sound didn't appear to originate from a particular source but rather materialised instantly in the crypt. It was closely followed by a foul breeze reeking of death and decay. "NOOO! JONATHAN. YOU ARE MINE! WE ARE MEANT FOR EACH OTHER. WE WILL BE TOGETHER, ALWAYS!". The image of the demonic entity appeared to be sitting in the coffin. Eric recoiled in fear. He didn't know if he would have the strength to fight her this time. Luck and the element had been on his side in the kitchen, here was her domain and her body. He would need to act fast or else he and Linda would be doomed. He thought of Linda and the rest was easy.

"You want your precious Jonathan? Here! Take him back you bitch!" Eric slammed the locket into the entity's chest. The spirit of the late Dame screamed again which devolved into a demonic howl. The crypt was filled with a cacophony of sound, the air filled with the sound of pain, agony and rage.

Then everything exploded.

Eric's last conscious thought was of flying marble, bone and skin. He sensed more than felt the large piece of rubble striking him on the head and knocking him to the floor. As he felt himself beginning to black out, he thought that as long as Linda was safe this wasn't the worst way to go.

Jail didn't turn out to be as bad as he had thought. The doctors hadn't thought him to be far gone enough to be committed but had recommended that he be in a secure unit with access to regular psychiatric evaluations. It seemed that having the reputation of a crazed man who single handedly tore up and aristocratic family's crypt with nothing, but a sledgehammer meant that the other inmates tended to give him a wide berth. He could have faced up to ten years, but his good character references, lack of criminal history and the Levin estate asking for leniency meant that he was only sentenced for a year. Out in six months providing good behaviour and a satisfactory psychiatric evaluation. He quickly settled into a routine and decided to turn his experience into a novella. He had never tried to be a writer before, so now seemed to be a good time.

The silence from Linda bothered him. Even though she never testified against him for the punch or went against what was generally said for his character references. She was conspicuously absent during the court proceedings. She didn't visit or write, nor did she send him anything in the way of comfort packages. The complete disengagement hurt Eric more than he could describe. Did she not remember the events leading up to that day? Had the spirit of Dame Levin warped her sense of reality so that he had a completely different recollection of events? He really wanted to know, or if nothing else hear from her to know that was okay. There weren't any papers served for divorce or protection orders issued so he still felt hope that things were salvageable. Maybe the shame of having her husband plastered over the newspapers as a deranged desecrator of graves was a bit much and she needed time to get over it. Some of her artist 'friends' wouldn't miss the opportunity to twist the knife a little over that to grab a rung above her in the social circle. He knew that much.

It was with surprise that with only a month left to serve Eric was called to the visitor's room. As he was led in, he was greeted by the sight of his wife. She almost looked business like in her knee length skirt, heels and pink blouse. Gone was the homespun artistic girl that he'd fallen in love with and married. He sat down across the table from her desperately wanting to reach out and hug her. To tell her that things were all right now.

She looked at him for a moment before speaking. "I'm sorry that I haven't been in touch. It was all a bit much you know." Eric nodded. "I understand honey, I don't blame you. Tell me. What do you remember?" Linda blushed slightly as she began to recall. "Only bits and pieces really. It was like a horrible nightmare. That's what took me the longest to deal with really. I had to give up the studio. Afterwards I completely lost my touch for pottery. I was breaking more than I was able to create and not to any decent standard. I sold my half to Patricia and went to work for an advertising agency. It's not horrible, and the days go in quickly."

Eric couldn't believe what he heard, Linda was an artist. It was in her blood. The last thing he could ever picture her doing was slaving away in the same type of corporate hell hole that he was accustomed to. He didn't even want to return to that life when he got out. Starting his writing journey had unlocked something in him and he wanted very much to continue exploring that when he returned to society.

"What happens now?" He asked, almost fearing to hear the answer. "I guess we start again." Linda answered. Eric's heart leapt for a moment at the prospect of rebuilding the home life they had again. Linda continued. "The Levin family felt bad about things for some reason. They acted very oddly about the whole affair. They sent us a bit of money to start up again, so I guess that will make things easier while we get back on our feet."

Eric couldn't help but smile as the buzzer signaled the end of visitation sounded. Eric stayed in his seat as he had been instructed to by the guards while Linda stood up. When she leant over to kiss him a locket slipped out from the top button of her blouse. The stone adorned piece of jewelry hung in the air on it's chain like a spectre coming back to haunt them. Linda smiled. "Don't worry Jonathan. We'll be together soon."

Follow Colin and his work here:

Thank you for taking the time to enjoy these stories. Please be sure to follow our authors by using the QR codes and pick up their work. Until next time our friends. Remember to keep it creepy, keep it HORRORific!

It's time to go on a HORRORific Journey!
HORRORific Tales
Volume Two (Crypids)
HORRORific Tales
Volume Three (Serial Killers)
(Volume 1)

Printed in Dunstable, United Kingdom

67901636R00137